STONECROP

The country I remember

BOOKS BY TEO SAVORY

NOVELS

Landscape of Dreams, *New York,* 1960
The Single Secret, *New York,* 1961; *London,* 1962
A Penny for the Guy, *London,* 1963; *New York,* 1964
To A High Place, *Santa Barbara,* 1972
Stonecrop: The Country I Remember, *Greensboro,* 1977

SHORT FICTION

A Clutch of Fables, *Greensboro,* 1977

POEMS

Traveler's Palm, 1967
Snow Vole, 1968
Transitions, 1973
Dragons of Mist and Torrent, 1974

TRANSLATIONS

ELEVEN VISITATIONS, katrina von hutten, *Munich,* 1971
(with Ursula Mahlendorf) THE CELL, Horst Bienek, *Santa Barbara*
and *Toronto,* 1972; *London,* 1974
SELECTED POEMS, Guillevic, *London* and *Baltimore,* 1973
EUCLIDIANS, Guillevic, *Greensboro,* 1975
(with Vo-Dinh) ZEN POEMS, Nhat Hanh, *Greensboro,* 1976

FOR THE UNICORN FRENCH SERIES

Supervielle, 1967
Corbière, 1967
Michaux, 1967
Queneau, 1971

Prévert I, 1967
Jammes, 1967
Prévert II, 1967
Guillevic, 1968

FOR THE UNICORN GERMAN SERIES

Günter Eich, 1971

Teo Savory

STONE

Unicorn Press

C R O P

The Country I Remember

ACKNOWEDGEMENTS

The poem by Trumbull Stickney (1874-1904) was suggested by
Edmund Wilson

The paragraphs about, and supposedly "from," the WPA Guide
Book in Section 17 were not suggested by the actual Guide,
and no offense is intended toward that worthy book or its
authors and editors

The story following that of "The Murdered Traveller" is authentic, but these particular incidents did not take place anywhere
near Afton County

Afton County is, in any case, located entirely in the author's
imagination, as are all its inhabitants, as well as its "narrator"

Sections 2 and 15 were both suggested by some prose, the first by
a passage in *Akenfield* by Ronald Blythe (Pantheon Books,
1969) and the latter by the heading (taken from a recording by
Ewan MacColl on *The Big Hewer*) of an article, "Coal The
Killer", by Paul J. Nyder, in *The Nation*, 20 September 1971

The author thanks Patricia Field, who gave up her time for the
author's writing time, and appreciates the help given by Fred
Chappell and David Martin.

UNICORN PRESS, INC.
Post Office Box 3307
Greensboro, North Carolina 27402

*To the memory of Will McCarthy
and to all New England friends and
neighbors, with esteem and affection*

...what I hear is the murmur
Of underground streams, what I see is a limestone landscape.

W. H. AUDEN

PRELUDE

AT THE SIDE OF THE ROAD

*As soon as you cross the town line from Afton to Stonecrop
there's no need of a sign to tell you so: the road gets
bumpy and narrow. The knobs of the Berkshire Hills grow
steeper and bolder, outcrops of marble are stark and grim.
The road's surface shows more patches than paving,
the shoulders are crumbled more often than not,
an old sign saying* Frost Heaves *hangs askew, a reminder
that though it's lush June now there was a snow-fall
last month, that before the corn in the roadside plots is
ripened frost might come soon enough to nip it.*

*The blind curve with a stone-shored side is all that's left
of an old railroad bridge. Round the curve there's the yellow
school bus. Four children hop off, skip down the road.
The bus driver waves, the children flap their satchels
at him: Goodbye, goodbye... Must be the last day of school.
Now there will be three months in the sun and the warm
summer rain, fishing in this brook, how swollen it is now,
must be from the melted snows, still melting up there
on Greystone Mountain, filling this brook and making it
leap over those rocks, making it churn under this rickety bridge.
There's an old man walking down the road with something
over his shoulder, looks like a scythe, the kind you see
in old pictures of Death the Grim Reaper or some such title,
but this old man looks harmless enough. Though he doesn't walk
so much as roll along on the outer edges of his feet. "Hello
there, old man, can you tell me the name of this brook?" (There's
wild flowers on the bank there, you can see the white fluff on
the Solomon's Seal, and a gaudy Jack-in-the-Pulpit beside
a pale, unfurling fiddlehead.) "Ain't got no name," he says.
What's that around his neck? Looks like a clove of garlic, what
peasants in remote Italian villages used to wear, sometimes,
to ward off the evil eye...*

1

But that was three thousand miles away and one hundred years ago, and this is the Commonwealth of Massachusetts in the later Twentieth Century, five miles from Afton, seat of the Summer Music Festival as well as of the County. Well, anyhow, he's rolled down the road now. His steel blade shoots bright darts back at the sun. Here come a few houses, three in a row, bungalows, fairly new, nothing to write home about in the way of architecture, he's rolling into the walk in front of the first one... Peonies are blooming on the edge of that lawn, and there's a maple with a bench underneath for shade. But where's the town? There's a hefty fellow, digging a ditch there, by the side of the road.

"Where's the town, where's Stonecrop?" He spits in a neat arc, and the spittle is dark brown. "You're in it," he says, and goes right back to digging. There's a pond, with a raft on it and some mown grass around it — looks like it was scythed. . . The water's sparkling but the place is empty. The sun's rays are slanting, there's a chill in the air... Better drive back to Afton, come up and try again in the morning.

1. THE POSTMASTER

CARL BARTUSHEK

Sure I can tell a lot of things about Stonecrop. You can always tell a lot about people by what letters they get, and what they say when they come in to buy stamps. Or mail a parcel — at Christmas, or to the old country, or something they got from the Catalogue that they want to send back... Besides that, I've lived here off and on since I was ten years old and father brought us here from Dorchester. Three hundred fifty people in the village and roundabout at the last census. Since then twenty-seven babies born, eighteen young men and fifteen girls went away, one old man came back, and nineteen people, nine of them babies, died. It almost evens out, but you see it shrinks some every year, and will even more, because pretty soon most all of the young ones will go. One of mine has already.

You could get all these facts from the so-called Town Hall — over there, see? — that wooden building with the flagpole in front of it. The Young Barber runs the flag up every morning and takes it down every night. I don't know why, he doesn't hold any office. Just he's always done it and his father before him. That building used to be an inn, there was a stop-over there on the Post Road once, so they say. When the Storekeeper's mother came here she took it over. I don't know what it was in between. Maybe empty, like lots of places. She made it a store and an eating-place, and rented the rooms upstairs. Now there's only the store. The rest of the downstairs is rented out to the Township, for the tax office, the *Sel*ectmen's office, and the library that's open twice a week, and the office for the Welfare. *That's* open every day.

I say you *could* get the statistics over there, but it wouldn't be easy. Town Hall's only open one or two evenings a month, and a lot of the old records are mislaid or stored away. Why, when my wife decided to take in lodgers during the Music Festivals and went to get her license, they couldn't even find the license book!

3

The thing to remember, first and last, is that this is a *poor* town.
It was settled in 1761 by some of the Yankees from Hartford
who'd gone to Afton and then came up here. The Hebberds and
Longyears are just about the only ones left of those first ten,
twelve families — and there aren't many of *them* now. They
owned all the land from Afton to the New York State line, and
they were well-to-do, I suppose you'd say, by the standards of
those days. Not rich, and the work must have been hard, but they
lived off the land, and lived well; they were independent. And
that's how it was for about a hundred years.

One day Old Man Longyear's grandpa was out walking his boundaries and caught his foot in a rabbit hole. Fell down and knocked
himself out. When he came to, he was lying across a patch of
rock the likes of which nobody'd ever seen hereabouts. He sent for
an expert, a geologist or the like, from Boston, and that's how the
iron ore was discovered. That's how the town began to change.
First there was the mining at the ore-bed, and the smelting in the
forge, and then there was the quarrying for the marble. So all the
poor from Boston and New York began to come to work for the
Longyears and the Hebberds and the others. Even came straight
here from the other side, like all the Toupences and a lot of those
Italians. So pretty soon us Outsiders — which was about the poli-
test thing they called us — far outnumbered the Yankees, but we
were kept down by our poverty and ignorance. It was still just
the way it was on the Other Side: the land-owners owned the
land and they owned us too.

The change came when they let their lands go fallow to get rich
— really rich, I mean, and without the hard work of farming —
from the mining and quarrying. But then the veins ran out, and
everybody was poor after that. Depression! — Hebberds even lost
their house. Over there — see? — that white Colonial on the rise
behind the privet hedge where the elm trees used to grow. The
Old Barber owns it now, Ghitalla, what these swamp Yankees
call a wop Yankee.

Well, that stuck in their craws! The town'd always been run by
Hebberds and Longyears, voting each other into office year after
year. But after that they just sort of dropped out, as my oldest

would say. Stayed home with their pride. Then the poor got their chance. Now two of our Selectmen have Italian last names and the third's a Mick, and here am I, a Slovak, the Postmaster.

But the town's run just as bad now as it was before. Then, from meanness. Now, from ignorance. Why, old Petrucca is drunk all the time and Foley most like can't even read. I and my family keep out of things. We worked hard to better ourselves and they could've done the same if they'd wanted to. My brother's head of the Young Democrats Club in Afton, and my sister's a school teacher. And take me, for instance. I went to the city and worked in a factory for ten years so I could go to night school and get my education. After I passed my Civil Service, I wasn't dependent on any ignorant Selectmen or anybody else. But they're not only ignorant — ignorance breeds corruption, as somebody said. Even this post office building itself, like that cracked sidewalk out there, is jerry-built from sheer graft. But that's another story. And no doubt the Hebberds have still another view of events. Of course, they still control Stonecrop because they own all the land, and they own the bank in Afton where us Outsiders get our mort-gages when we buy a few acres. They own the grain and hard-ware store, too, on Maple Street, and I guess you could hear a lot from Old Hebberd or his son the Deacon, if they wanted to talk. Which isn't likely.

A busy post office? Yes, I'd say it's that. This Township con-sists of Cobday's Corners (though there's no born Cobdays live there now), Mill Hollow, the Massachusetts side of State Line, and the village itself. Once there was Brandon's Corners, too, but we don't have to service that area, there's nobody there now. Here's the map they ought to have over at the Town Hall but probably don't. Most of the inhabited houses are marked on it. You'll notice I say inhabited, not necessarily habitable . . . To get to the Cor-ners you go south back along the road you doubtless drove up on, to the far end of the Pond; Mill Hollow is down below there to your right going south, centered around the bridge over the West Afton River (which some call a creek), not far from the old quarry. From there the road goes up the mountain where there's a few dwellings, and changes into a cart track that goes over the mountain and ends up at State Line.

There's others know more than I do here: they're older, some
have lived here all their lives. The Old Barber, for instance. Or
Emmet McSorley. He's like me, self-educated. But he never bet-
tered himself by it. In any case, I close up the office from twelve
to two to go home for my dinner, and there goes the noon whistle.
A room for the summer? No, I don't know of any.

Did you know that this village used to be called West Afton? It
was the old-time farm laborers that named it Stonecrop, and that's
its legitimate name today on the rolls of the United States Postal
System.

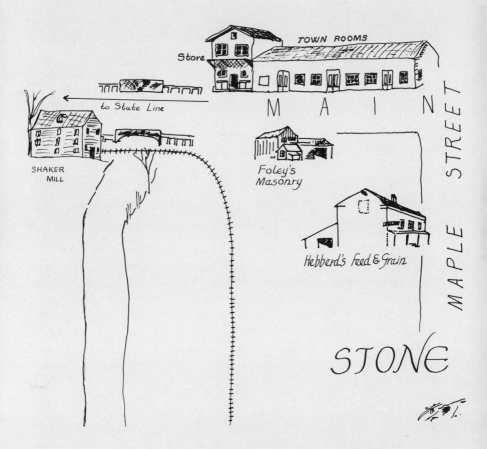

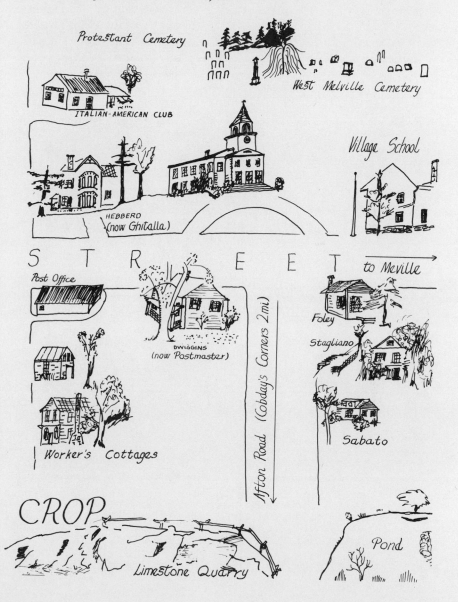

↑ to Longyear house and farm

Protestant Cemetery

West Melville Cemetery

ITALIAN-AMERICAN CLUB

Village School

HEBBERD
(now Ghitalla)

S T R E E T

to Meville

Post Office

DWIGGINS
(now Postmaster)

Foley

Stagliano

Afton Road (Cobday's Corners 2mi)

Worker's Cottages

Sabato

CROP

Limestone Quarry

Pond

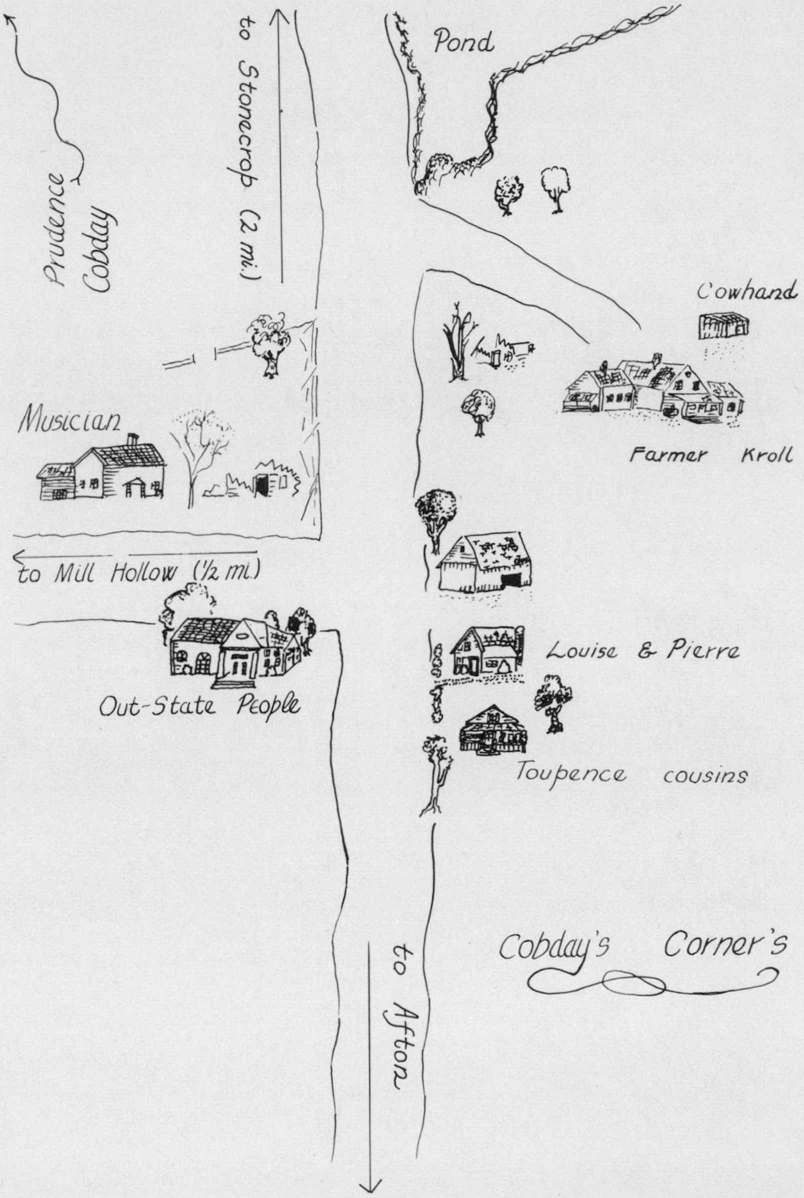

to Stonecrop (2 mi.)

Prudence Cobday

Pond

Musician

Cowhand

Farmer Kroll

to Mill Hollow (½ mi.)

Out-State People

Louise & Pierre

Toupence cousins

to Afton

Cobday's Corner's

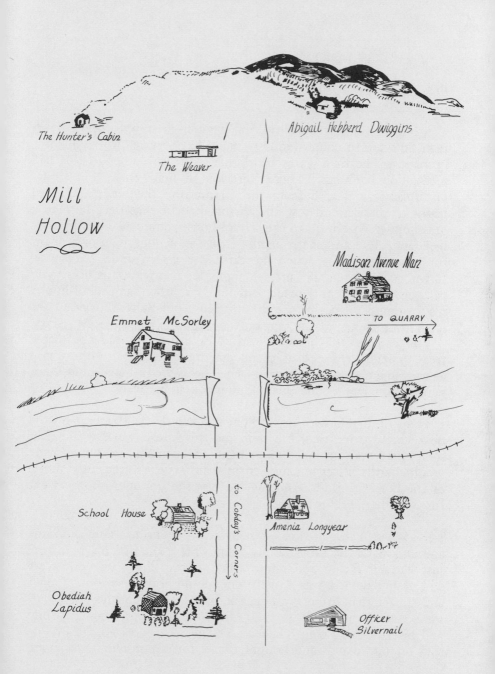

The Hunter's Cabin

Abigail Hebberd Dwiggins

The Weaver

Mill
Hollow

Madison Avenue Man

Emmet McSorley

TO QUARRY

School House

Amenia Longyear

Obediah
Lapidus

Officer
Silvernail

to Coblay's Corners

2. THE WIDOW

PRUDENCE COBDAY

Yes, I've been twice a widow, and lived alone now for more years than I'd want to count. Nobody could have wished for two better husbands. The first was a handsome lad. Our father's fields had a common boundary. There were lots of fields then. The stones our forebears cleared from the earth made the fences. My lad learnt to plough and sow the earth when he was knee-high to a grasshopper. We went to the school-house together. The big brass bell rang clear and sharp on the frosty mornings. We only went for lessons, you see, when the earth was asleep under the snow. It was painted red, the little school, just the way it is now, you can see it cross-lots a piece, only it's not now the school-house, it's a summer place for a rich lady from out-State. They say she used to be an actress and act on the stage in the city. — My stars! — You can see the brass bell still hanging there, and the maple trees in front, thirteen of them, one for each state of the union at the time they were planted. Their leaves will be turning color before you can count them. Summer's soon over.

I lay in the fields with my lad the summer I was sixteen, and the next year we married. He built me this house, my lad did. But soon there was no more of a living to be made, what we grew would hardly bring enough for the next year's seed, any more, or the horses' fodder. And my lad was the youngest. So he went for a soldier. His grave is across the ocean.

I lived best I could. Then I married his cousin, about the same age and with the same family name. He ploughed his land too, just like his father and grandfather before him. We both were still young then, I was a lively one, could always step out longer and spryer than anyone else at the barn dance, and he was handsome too like my first lad. But the same hard time come to him and his land. We sold our team and let the acres go fallow, we sold off our woods and bought cattle. But we couldn't get along

10

even so. The harder we worked the less we had, and a sickness came over the cattle. So my man took off to find better times for us, went for a cowhand in Texas. I waited here to be sent for. But I never was.

My man was kicked in the side by a horse and he died of it. He too lies in far-away earth.

Men should die where they lived.

3. THE WOODCUTTER & HIS WIFE

ANGELO & CATARINA SABATO

Go in the cellar old man to smoke that pipe

She don' like no smoke in her kitchen, è vero, but when I
walk home from scythin down by the pond I like to sit by warm
stove   I look at the red coals and smell the coffee the woman
is makin   My blades come from Austria and I keepin them sharp
myself   See how they're thin now and sharp sharp   Scythin the
grass by Longyear Pond so molti ragazzi go swim there   But
more rocks than grass there   big rocks little rocks breakin
my blade sometimes   Nobody know no more how to scythe
I teachem Antonio but now he goin away

Antonio no want to be Antonio old man   He Tony now he goin
fine school in city   He no need to learnem scythe   goin to
college   My grandson

No I never went swim in this pond nor no other   Only workin
Work tutta la vita   Age o' ten workin in fields in Italia
Age o' twenty goin to war in Italia   Age o' twenty-five comin
here live on Greystone Montagna   woodchopper   cuttin trees
makin logs   summer and winter   Many many men from my villagio
Built our own huts from the logs we cut down   In summer mosquitoes   in winter molto frío   the snow she sometimes ten feet
sometimes fifteen   Then I come to this town gettin job clearin
stones outa fields   my compaesani gettin jobs in the quarry
No limestone quarry those days: marble quarry   Then I get
little shack in villagio and send for the woman   Now
we got house warm nice   Got a well for the water   pipe to
the sink   But I'm old now my feet don' go any more
Too late to enjoy   Whatsa difference, stay in Italia
come here?

Old man forgets but talkin too much

12

No I never went back   The woman once she went back   Why
you're callin me Mr Sabato?   *Mister* Sabato gottem good feet
wore shoes all his life lies in bed sleepin at sun-up
Angie Sabato get up at five goin to work all his life

Go to the cellar old man smoke your pipe
Now I tell you: old man he don't remember so good   Me
I remember   In our villagio in Italia we all livin in caves
Too poor for houses   Own nothin   No house no shoes no fields
Workin in other man's fields   Too poor for house livin in caves
School maybe two three years then go to work   Old man sure
he work hard all his life but now see our warm house   See
our grandson Tony   he goin to school then he goin to
college be a big man   I takin in wash savin money   Tony
he goin to fight in Vietnam justa like all American boys
He American boy   Then he come back and I givem the money
for college   America good   Italia no good   Tony born
in America

No my old man   he don't remember

4. THE CITY BOY

ORDI KRANTZ

We came here in this old Saab I borrowed me and my friends
seven of us
Drove up from the city and just cruised around
Heard there was an old marble quarry
filled up with water   Lotta kids skinny
dipping and laying around on the marble slabs
in the sun blowing grass kind of cold up here
though   So we drove around some more
down this dirt road see kind of bumpy
couldn't find anything   Saw an old
white house behind a lot of trees
white wooden house and a man   Kind of
an old man up on a ladder wow high
up painting white paint on these old
boards like up on the peak there
so we shouted at him like Man is there
an old quarry around here? Hell no!
he said kind of snarling   So we drove
off man did we drive and drive bumpy roads
and nothing but trees all over the place
Everybody we asked said, at least some
did a lot didn't answer like at all, well
they told it was back there down a path
near where that man was painting this
big old wooden house   So we drove back
and there he was still up there on this ladder
Man we said we *know* there's a quarry to
swim in around here   Now you just tell us
where's that path? He shinned down off
that high ladder awful quick for an old
guy   He had this paint brush in his hand

14

must of been about a foot across and he
run up to the old Saab and shook a lot of
this white paint all over everything and he said:
Men *died* in that quarry   So we drove
back to this town Afton they call it and tomorrow we'll
go back to the city   That old man can keep his quarry
and the country too

5. THE HOUSE PAINTER

OBEDIAH LAPIDUS

Ayeh, I was born right over there in that white cottage where Amenia Longyear lives now, and went to school right here in this school-house. Got to get the underpinnings fixed up on this here porch before I can paint it. See where that dratted porcupine gnawed it? It was a hungry winter, this one past, for deer and rabbit and porcupine alike, and for some men too. Guess that porcupine would've gnawed the whole thing away if I hadn't of shot him. Porch wouldn't of been no loss, to my mind, as a school-house never had no porch. But it's Miss Dilworth's summer place now, and if she wants a porch, she can have a porch. Got to get these underpinnings shored up real speedy now, afore she gets here, as she herself ain't too steady at times on her *own* under-pinnings, if you take my meaning.

Ayeh, all of us that was born down here in the Hollow, and nearby at the Corners as well, went here to school at one time or another: me, and Emmet McSorley, and the Toupences; also Angie Sabato's son and all them other Italians that later got killed in the marble quarry. The Hebberds and all of that lot went to the big school up on Main Street in the village proper. But Abigail Hebberd, she that's the Widow Dwiggins now, she taught here my last year, wasn't much older'n me or that Sabato fellow, and did we give *her* a lively time of it... After we grew too old, and I might say too big as well, to come here, we all took the train that used to run from over to Albany in New York State and past our quarry and down all the way to Connecticut. Don't run no more now, though you can still see the tracks down there alongside the river. What's left of them. (There's many a shed or porch round here firmed up with railroad ties 'stead of two-by-fours.) But in those days there was a sign by the bridge, one of those Stop Look and Listen crosses, and underneath another sign reading Mill Hollow, and that's where the train stopped and blew its whistle every morning eight o'clock sharp and we all piled on into the one and

16

only passenger car, which was already near filled with Hebberds and Longyears, and some Varconis and Ghitallas and Foleys too, and rode down to Afton High School.

Ayeh, born right over there, and when I'd got my growth and learned my trade and got married, I built me that cottage yonder that you can't see too good through the spruce trees, and that's where I live to this day.

Me and my wife like all them evergreens. Makes the front room dark, but keeps folks from prying and spying. There was this scandal, see, which I do not aim to talk about, when we got married — not even in no church, neither! — and folks around here got nothing to do all winter but gossip and keep old grudges burning. Why, one time John Toupence, Pierre's cousin that later got killed in the quarry, spent the whole winter building a spite shack across the road from the old house he'd been born in that some out-State folks'd bought, so it was the first thing they'd see when they looked out their front windows. Mighty fierce winter that year. That shack fell down under the weight of the snow, and John got his fingers frost-bit.

My house, now, it stands as straight and true as the day it was built. Emmet McSorley taught me a lot of what he knew when I was a boy. You can see even through the trees how straight the ridge-pole is. Them six-by-eights at the four corners was twenty feet high and weighed about a hundred and fifty pounds apiece, and I put 'em all in place myself. My wife's brother, that hadn't spoke to us for two years, come along and offered his help. I said, I don't need help from no man under God's heaven.

Ayeh, yonder cottage is where I was born, here's where I went to school, and over there's my house. You could say: Obediah Lapidus was born in the Hollow, always lived in the Hollow, and that's where he'll be buried. At least that's how I always thought it would be.

But the world, or maybe 'twas the U. S. Government, ruled otherwise.

You see these deep creases in my face? They was put there by fierce tropical suns.

The war come along, is what happened. Folks around here never had time for knowing about the rest of the world. Things weren't easy then like they are now. It was all a man could do to keep himself and his family alive through a winter. So what could we, here in Stonecrop, know of Germans or Japs? Pearl Harbor was a place we'd never heard of and didn't know where it was. When we found out, many among us asked what was our ships doing there anyhow on some island that belonged to folks that wasn't even white?

Hardly anybody wanted to go. One of the Ghitallas, when he got drafted, went so far as to cut off his own toe.

Me and two others got sent to the South Pacific. The Old Barber said there'd be a lot of beautiful island girls out there, half-naked and giving a handsome young soldier bananas and coconuts and a lot of other things too.

Well, it wasn't like that at all. The island I was at, all the women was *black*.

There was a lot of Limeys there too. We couldn't understand their speech, and they laughed at ours. Before we went, the Reverend up at the Meeting House — I hadn't set foot in it since before my marriage, but I went along that one time, for some reason or other — he told us how we were going to protect our country and the glory of our flag, and also have what he called a broadening experience.

I didn't find it so. As for the other two that went with me, one got killed, and the other one lives in a dirty old shack and's never drawn a sober breath since. And me? Well, you see this finger? Rather, where this finger *ain't?* You might think I got it caught in a bear-trap or mangled it with a hammer. Not so. Piece of flak hit it. Freakish, eh? There was quite an investigation: U. S. Army don't believe in freakish occurrences. Finally decided I was telling the truth, though, and I got sent home with my good name and minus half of one finger, and half a year afore anybody else.

Howsomever, I might just as likely have mashed it in my work, and I get a little bit of disability pension, so I'd say the outcome was in my favor. Specially as it don't impede me in my work.

But that's not what I meant — about what kind of "experience" that was. All I know is, I missed out four whole years of my life, four turns of the seasons from winter to spring. My corn-patch got full of weeds, and my goat died, and my wife got broody.

No, I *don't* agree with them hippies — dirty, smelly, good-for-nothings. They think those yellow Chinks is their brothers. Now I ask you, isn't that stupid? Don't agree with Emmet McSorley and his world government stuff neither. This country should keep to itself. Let the rest of the world go to hell in a high basket if it wants to. We should keep out of it. Isn't that what our founding fathers said?

All I know is, I should've stayed right here where I was born and raised, that was my plan and what I was meant to do. Going far away like that was unsettling.

The West Afton marble quarry, which was discovered in 1820 by Major C. Longyear, the then owner of the land, began to be mined by an outside company which leased the mineral rights for ninety-nine years, in 1821. The site was part of a government land grant originally acquired by Joshua Codwise in 1792, which grant extended from the southern bank of the West Afton River at its source in the village of Stonecrop (then West Afton) in a southerly direction to the northern boundary of Afton Township, following the river from its source to said boundary, where it joins the Hoosac, and including lands on either side of it in extent varying from ten rods to roughly two miles. The large outcrop of marble was discovered on top of the hill or mountain, rising about midway between Stonecrop village and the Afton Township line, known as Mother Ann's Mountain.*

Marble was quarried successfully and profitably from the site for well over one hundred years, and gave employment to over half the inhabitants of the village of Stonecrop. The marble was, unlike the pink-veined or pure white type of stone found in Vermont, mostly of a greyish cast and therefore considered by some experts to be second-grade. Its durability, however, enabled it to be easily milled without cracking or chipping, and also made it impervious to erosion by weather conditions, so that, commercially, it was found

---

*During the brief stay of "Mother Ann" (the founder of the "Shaker" movement) and some of her disciples in Stonecrop, it is said that one night, several Townsmen attempting to drive her away by threats and burning crosses, she took refuge, in fear for her life, in a cave on this mountain. The tale has proved completely apocryphal as well as, probably, anachronistic, but the name given the hill persists.

to be superior to the Vermont variety. It had many uses, from the construction of imposing civic buildings in New York, Philadelphia and Melville (Mass.), to its more homely use as doorsteps in city and country dwellings and as counter-tops in the then ubiquitous soda-fountains.

The mining was begun in tunnels in the sides of the mountain, and continued in depth through many rich veins until the level of the surrounding pasture-land had been reached, at which time the central area of the mountain had been quarried to a width of thirty feet, almost to the endings of the veins. However, even richer veins were found below the level of the surrounding flat lands, and the mining continued as briskly as before.

For the first forty-eight years, the marble was mined entirely by hand, pushed on carts to the edge of the river and there, a towpath having been constructed, loaded onto ox-drawn barges and hauled downstream to the Afton plan-ing-mill, thence taken by ox-cart either to the Hudson or the Hoosac Rivers for further transport. After the building of the Hartford, Hoosac and Albany Railroad, a spur of the tracks (known colloquially as "the switcher") was built on the site of the towpath and the marble was then transported by rail.

On March 17, 1936, at eleven o'clock in the morning, when the work below ground (some say forty, some fifty, feet down: as the records were lost, this cannot be ascertained with any accuracy) was in full swing, one wall of the quarry collapsed from the pressure, behind it, of an underground spring, and the mine filled up with water in a matter of sec-onds. There were no survivors. No bodies were recovered, but it is assumed from the timekeeper's daily record sheet* (and by the later non-appearance of the workmen on his list) that the following inhabitants of Stonecrop were killed in the disaster:

---

*The life of Thomas Parnell McSorley, the Timekeeper, was spared, due to his having regarded March 17, St. Patrick's Day, as a national holiday and having left the premises at 6:30 a.m. after checking in the other workmen.

Obediah Lapidus (the Elder), *Superintendent*
"Dynamiter" Cayuno (first name not recorded)
Pietro Varconi
Jonas Codwise
Joseph John Foley
Enrico Ghitalla
Giulio Ghitalla
Thomas Halloran
Luca Zavatino
John Toupence
Bobbie Bouchard
Sam Petrucca
Mario Stagliano
Enrico Stagliano
Arcangelo Sabato
Marcantonio Mazzeo
Emanuel Mazzeo
Enrico Mazzeo
Rosario di Cecco
Joe Sarasate
Pasquale Quaglino
Riccardo Sobrani
Artie Hanzlichek
Zbigniew Chesloff
1 transient (name not recorded)

Existing reports by Obediah Lapidus (the Elder) were discovered, which contained increasingly emphatic complaints concerning the seepage of water from the north wall of the mine, and an investigation was begun by Commonwealth officials, but no evidence could be found.

As there was no provision made by the owners for what would now be termed "Workmen's Compensation," or life insurance, the surviving relatives of the dead made complaints to the State Legislature, but no indemnity was found to be owing.

Since 1936 no further marble quarrying has been undertaken in the Township of Stonecrop, although several promising sites were known to exist, due to the fact that the market for marble, already on the decline, had diminished to the point where quarrying was no longer profitable. In the same year, the spur of the railroad was also abandoned.

6. THE DRAFT GENERATION

ANTONIO SABATO

VINCE STAGLIANO

FRANK FOLEY

A HITCH-HIKER

Antonio Sabato

That's all very well, about my being such a fine American boy and going into the army and kill off the Vietnamese with all those other fine American boys! Old Noni, my grandmother I mean, she's a stubborn old woman, though I don't hold it against her. How else could she have survived, the life she's had? But she's got so many ideas in her head about what I am and what I'm going to do, and they're nearly all of them wrong. Nothing I can say — in English *or* Italian — can change her mind. That's one of her misconceptions: that I don't want to speak Italian. It's good to have another language, brings you closer to other people somewhere else in the world. And Italian! — that's Dante's language... And then she thinks I want to change my name to Tony. I *like* my name. Then there's what I've learned from my grandfather. All I ever learned was from one class in school, and from him. Maybe more from him. But you'd never get her to see that. He taught me all the wood-lore I know, all the skills and crafts that are getting lost, dying out. But I'm trying to teach them myself, now, to the little kids around here, and I'll go on with that when I come back.

What's poor old Noni going to do when I go to prison? Her biggest mistake was to send me to school! There I read history. I read Italian history. But mostly I read American history. People came over here to get away from wars and killing. I read the Constitution. That's more than Vince ever has, or a lot of other people, including most of our teachers. If all men are created free and equal, then all men are brothers. The Vietnamese are my brothers too. "If we kill our brothers, with whom shall we live?" So that's why I'm going to prison.

23

Nobody knows about it yet. I'll spare Noni as long as I can, but that's all I can do... Nobody except my grandfather. I don't know how it is, but he seems to understand what I have to do. And when my term's over, I'll come back here. Right now we're fixing up this abandoned building, the old Forge, for our future headquarters, a clubhouse for the summer camp we're planning. Day camp for Stonecrop boys and girls. Free, of course. It's just a small beginning. We won't be able to use it in the winter, when there's even more need for a place. But anything's better than what they have now. Hang around outside the barber shop in summer, break into the summer people's places in the winter. Smoke pot at the old quarry — boy from Afton just got drowned there. But nobody does anything. It's we who got the idea of making the old ore bed into the town pond. But even after we'd raised most of the money for it, it took three years to get the Selectmen moving. But a kid can't swim all year round, or even all day long in summer. Now that there's no arable land for them to work on — and if there were, they wouldn't work like slaves on it the way our fathers or grandfathers did — they don't know anything about the earth they walk on. No wonder all they do is hang around and get in trouble, waiting for the time when they can leave.

Yes, I'll have plenty to do. When I come back.

*   *   *   *

Vince Stagliano

Tony's full of crap. Right up to his ears. Best thing to do about this town is to get out of it. Best way to get out of it is to get drafted. What's he all worked up about a bunch of coloreds for, anyhow? Who cares? Just so long as you shoot first. Anyhow, I figured it all out two years ago. I got out of that fancy new High School they send us to in Afton. I went to Poly in Albany and now I'm a licensed mechanic — not just cars, either, trucks, tractors, you name it. So I won't get sent any place dangerous. I'll be some place safe working on engines. And plenty of pay in my pants. What's the difference, so long as you get away? Tony ought to wise up. What's he want to go to prison for, what did these stupid "brothers" of his ever do for him? And before he

goes to prison he's in for a lot of trouble — his old Noni scream-
ing the place down, the priest yacking at him every day, and the
whole town turning against him. He thinks he can come back
here? That's a laugh. He'll just be a jailbird to all of them, same
as my old man's cousin was when he got caught ripping off the
town tax-money. After he got out, nobody'd have anything to
do with him, and he had to go out-State. All the rest of the Selectmen were doing the same thing, but *they* didn't get caught.
I learned my lesson early: that no man's your brother, and the
only one to look out for you is yourself. Tony, it seems, never
learned *nothing*.

And I can tell you one thing for sure — him and Frank aren't
going to suck me into this clubhouse building crap any longer.
Look at them, hauling rocks around! Why should I get in a
sweat for a bunch of dumb kids? Let them get along the same
way I had to.

If Tony doesn't want to get drafted, why don't he go to Canada?
Like the Postmaster's son? Those Polack Bartusheks, think they're
better than anybody else, now the laugh's on them — they got a
draft-dodger in the family! But that kid was smarter than Tony,
anyhow.

But what's really smart is to get yourself a good safe job in the
army, it's good pay and the best way to get out of here.

* * * * *

Frank Foley

We're building the fireplace now. Fieldstone's nice, isn't it? My
father's a mason, that's how I know how to build it. We drag the
stones up from that old dry wall down by the road. Kids like a
fire, you know. But I don't know if we'll have time to finish.

Antonio's got more courage than I have. On the other hand, he's
got a better chance to go through with his decision than I'd
ever get. His folks are dead, and though his grandma's going to
make an awful fuss when she finds out, Antonio will be in Boston
by then, waiting for his trial. We talked things over a lot when we
first started High School. Luke Hebberd was sent away to some

snobby prep-school, where he learned about Conscientious Objection and the draft laws, and when he came back — guess he got expelled from there, too — he told us about all that. None of us even knew there is such a thing as a 1-0 Classification till then. So Antonio and I talked it over, heard about the Quakers' place in Philadelphia where you can get draft counseling, and even cut school once and hitched down there. We found out more, and made up our minds. We even found out about the Vigil — you know? Every Wednesday noon, all over the world, almost, people stand in silence together, and maybe prayer, to protest the War. We even had one in Stonecrop. Were we the dumb innocents! Had it under the flagpole. Five of us. Vince was different then, he was there. Luke Hebberd too, though he didn't stay long. Anyhow, the young barber's sons and their friends came along and beat us up. And that was the end of *that*. Only for me it was just the beginning. All that my folks care about is getting to be lace-curtain Irish instead of shanty Irish. And part of that endeavor has to be me and what I do. They want me to go to college, they want me to go to R.O.T.C., they want me to go in the army. My ma's even blood-thirstier than my pa. "I'd rather have a gold star than a dirty draft-dodger," she said after she found out. Then the priest came. He said the Vigil was communist and that Quakers are heretics, and that Gandhi was a heretic *and* a communist. And that I've got to go fight for my country. My pa simply gave me a hiding.

Anyhow, Antonio and I went ahead and when the time came we both applied for C.O. status. There was just the two of us by then. Vince changed his mind, and Luke was exempted anyhow, and our other friend took off for Canada. We haven't been investigated yet; anyhow, Antonio decided he couldn't accept *any* kind of service. He says, "From a wrong government waging a wrong war, you can accept nothing." Antonio knows these things, you see. He's read history and Gandhi and all. I just haven't the head for learning. So he joined the Resistance. I'm still waiting to get my 1-0, but what's the chances? You have to have people say you're a sincere Objector. Well, who's going to do that? My folks, the priest, that High School principal? There's only the history teacher, Mr. Endicott, but he's left here, got in some kind of trouble, I heard.

No, I don't know how it'll turn out. Maybe I'll take off for Canada, like the Postmaster's son, maybe I'll go to New York and get lost like some do, maybe I'll end up in jail with Antonio!

But I know I could never come back here. Antonio wants me to promise to come back and finish this clubhouse, and go on with our plans. I'd never be able to face that. All the meanness and prejudice in this town. Like I said, Antonio's got more courage than I have.

* * * * *

A Hitch-hiker

Thanks for stopping, mister. There's not many do around here. Scared of long-hairs. Well, I'm scared of them bald-heads. I got to go to Afton every Monday to report to my probation officer and a meaner old bastard I never met. Most weeks I have to walk there *and* back. I got a car, see, but they took away my license. Only another month now, though, and I'm through. Then they won't see me around here for shit.

What for? Nothing that great. All those Staglianos and Ghitallas get their kicks breaking into houses and busting everything up. I just like to drive around, get out of here a ways. Maybe park someplace quiet for an hour. I was speeding, see, down that new strip of road by the Corners, and that stupid fuzz Silvernail caught me.

Found a couple of joints in the car. Big deal! But another month, and I can just drive away.

No, I don't go to school. I quit some time back. What was there in that school for me? No, I don't work, neither. What's the point? You could say I'm waiting around. For something. Whatever it is.

The Army'll have to catch me first, won't they? But I guess I'll go if they do. What's the difference?

Right down there in the trailer-court, next to the Dump, that's where I live. If you can call it that.

Thanks for the lift, mister.

7. THE WIDOW WHO CAME BACK

LOUISE TOUPENCE GOODHUE

We were born, Pierre and me, in that white clapboard farmhouse across the road. This place was the tenant farmer's house. The five houses here at the Corners were all on our land in those days. This one's not very pretty, is it, but Pierre worked himself half to death to get this part of the old property back again. Now it's his, free and clear, house, barn and five fields. Our folks lost their house and lands in the Depression. But I'd gone away by then anyhow. I went to the city to try my luck. I apprenticed myself to a hairdresser — that's why some of us old girls along Afton Plains Road have nice blue rinses and pretty soft waves or French twists, instead of going around straggly-haired or neck-clipped like those fat Italian women. I just do that for fun, I don't need the money. After I'd been in the city a while, I met Doctor, and we married. We lived in peace and harmony for twenty years, and then he was taken. One minute rushing down to the hospital on an emergency case, the next dropping dead in the doorway of the operating room. Oh we had better than peace and harmony: we had fun. I couldn't grow my flowers and vegetables in a city backyard, so I made beer. It was Prohibition days then, you see. Of course I baked and preserved, just like here, and made clothes and quilts and all that, but the beer was something special. People used to drive to our neighborhood from all over and then start asking around. Doctor was well-known for being a specialist in liver ailments. (Pierre could certainly do with some treatment like that, he's such a bad-humored old codger, must be his liver.) Well, those people were never asking around for Doctor's house, though — they always asked, Where's the Beer Lady? That used to make him laugh. He had such a hearty laugh...

Then there was my rugs. Doctor designed them and I hooked them out of rags I'd saved. This one here, for instance, these three Indians in their war-paint sneaking across the Housatonic

28

River in their canoe. And then this one, Washington crossing the Delaware. Oh it's all right to walk on them, that's what they're for. The Weaver, that lives up-mountain now, wanted to get them in a show in some museum, but I'd rather have them here with me. Of course I don't let Pierre put his dirty feet on them: I don't let him nor his crony that clumsy McSorley in this front parlour at all. Now take this one, Paul Revere's Ride, for instance. Doctor designed that dark, electric-blue sky to show it was night. He had a suit with two pairs of pants, one pair of which being wore out, they became the sky. (Those little pin-point stars were my good yellow silk blouse once upon a time.) Well, just when I got to that northeast corner, I ran out of blue. Doctor came home to lunch as usual, and as he came in the door I saw what suit he was wearing... "Doctor," I said, "you just take those pants right off and give them to me." That's what I mean by we had fun.

Doctor was a fine bold figure of a man. But he was taken in his prime. We always had more fun than money — though I did have my mink cape, and if this was church-time on Sunday you'd see me wearing it, to the eternal bedazzlement of Stonecrop — so I had to sell Doctor's and my house. But I still had my savings — from those Prohibition days — and now I have my pension. But I was awful lonely. Pierre's wife died. I guess he worked her to death. So I came back here where I'd started from, to keep house for Pierre. His son lived here then too, I looked after the both of them. ...Oh no, he's long since gone to California. We've never set eyes on him since.

Pierre doesn't bother *me* with his bad-tempered ways and his dirty mouth. He's got his heifer to look after — he's real fond of that heifer — and his vegetable patch and his chickens, and now that he's got his pension, too, he's filled our old barn up with junk that he calls antiques. He and his crony can set outside there in their rockers all summer and watch the tourists go by and sometimes even sell something. Pierre's had a rough life. He had to quit school when he was eleven, and work like a plough horse ever after. That's what makes *him* so rough. After the farm was lost, he went to work for the paper factory in Melville as a truck-driver, till he lost his eye — a hook from the conveyor-belt ran into it — then as a farmhand for the Longyears. Worked half his life there, living in Longyear's leaky old tenant house. He never had any chance to educate himself, the way I did, and he married a Toupence cousin, just as ignorant as he was.

There he is now, the old goat, out pulling up my flowers along with the weeds. But he looks after me in his own way, and I have this place the way I want it. I can cook for him, and bake for the church suppers. I make quilts, too, and sell them through that Craft Guild in Afton. No, I don't make any more rugs. Who'd make the designs?

I've had a good, full life, and I'm ending my days the best way anyone could; I don't regret a thing.

8. THE FIELD-HAND

PIERRE TOUPENCE

Planting peas is damn worse on your back than weeding. You got to make long, even drills, plant each seed one inch apart — seeds cost money — then hill 'em up. There's no machinery can do it right. Got to plant plenty, too, so as to have a nice mess of early ones, small and juicy, along with your first spring lamb. Used to keep a few sheep, only got the heifer now. Blackie I call him. Back gets tired weeding, too. Old back, old bones. Best go and set now in front of the barn. Have to keep working hard while the weather lasts. Summer's short here. Last year snow fell in May. Frost comes in September. Some years ain't even enough weeks between killing frosts so as you can get your tomatoes and corn in. Fellow I met in Florida didn't even know what a killing frost is. Damn ignorant fool. That's what they all are down there, with their bathing-suits and their sunshine. Talk funny there, too, can't hardly understand them. Ayeh, Louise dragged me down to that Florida one winter after my woman died.

But nice to set here in front of the barn in our mountain sunshine. Don't last long, though, like I said. Gets dark around three, four o'clock come November. This here's my rocker and that's the one Emmet McSorley uses. He knows about antiques. Found a lot of 'em right in our own house, him and Louise did. Who'd ever thought that old wash-stand where I sluiced myself down of a freezing cold morning would fetch a hundred dollars? The folks that bought it wouldn't know what to do if they had to wash theirselves at it. — Probably made it into a drinking-bar. Fact is, the city people that just bought the old Codwise place, they bought that wash-stand. Folks are soft now, got to have gas stoves, washing machines, drilled wells and pumps, stuff that's always breaking down, modern inconveniences...and heat they got to have in every room. Soft! When me and Lou was kids, there was the kitchen stove to warm yourself at and, on Sundays,

31

the cast-iron pot-belly in the parlour. Winter evenings, we'd toast ourselves in the kitchen, one side then the other, then run up and get between them cold sheets. Rooms up there was so cold the piss used to freeze in the pots.

Ayeh, city folks is soft. But they buy a lot of old stuff we reckon's only fit to throw out. Me and Emmet goes to auctions every week, he knows what's wanted, like I said, then him and Lou scrapes the paint off of the furniture and oils it, and I sell it to them city people. Emmet buys a lot of glass and china, but I don't mess with breakables, he sells that stuff out of his own house. Me, I buy a lot of harness, sell the brasses off of it. Don't know what they want that stuff for, ain't no horses no more, maybe they hang it over their wash-stands? Piece of good harness weighs about a hundred pounds. And my truck there, see, she's got a high tailboard. But Emmet's gone flabby since he don't get up on his high roofing ladders no more. He's got swollen joints. Younger'n me, too, by six months. Can't bend his knees to set down, has to go flop. Busted one of Lou's damn old Shaker chairs, floppin', now she won't let him in the parlour no more. So, Emmet being no use, I got me one of them Stagliano kids to come along to barn auctions — about fifteen he is, big strong wop kid. But these kids now is all soft like city folks. Here he comes now, riding that high-falutin bike his ma bought him. (I'd of made him work for it.) Can't even walk a quarter-mile down-street, gotta ride, look at him toting his kid brother on the handle-bars. — Hey, boy, don't you know you'll break your brother's balls, toting him like that? —

Take them Shakers now — folks've got a fad for their chairs of late — they didn't have no balls. Or if they did, didn't use 'em. Furniture's all very well, but a man needs his pleasures too.

Emmet says I don't understand about them Shakers. Huh! There's plenty I don't know about. Never had no education. Know how to grow corn though. Emmet's smart, smarter'n me beyond a doubt, but always got his nose in a book, can't make no money that way.

French accent? How could I have any French accent? Toupences have lived in Afton County since way before the Civil War. My grandfather had a place here where he hid out slaves that was escaping to Canada. Mr. Lincoln sent him a signed picture of hisself. Wonder Lou didn't show it to you, always shows it. Lou was always at me to take a trip to France to see where we stemmed from. But I already know about that. Reason the Toupences is here is because of the Forge. First Forge in Afton County, smelted the ore from Longyear's Ore Bed. It was fired by charcoal. The poorest of the poor in France is them that lives in the woods and is charcoal-burners. That's why Grandpa was glad enough to come here, and after he got his land grant, to send for all his relations. Now there's a hundred families of us up and down Afton Plains Road, all related. Why would I want to go back there? In Europe all they got is wars and hatred. All different nations with different languages fighting each other. Kind of like Hebberds and Longyears fighting over boundaries. I don't dispute I'm uneducated and can't put my mind to reading, but I figured out long ago what's needed, and that's one government for the whole world. Even for those wops and black Africans. So why should I want to go to France? I've hauled rocks and ploughed the earth and shovelled snow as long as any Yankee. — You want to hear some French accents, you go talk to Frenchie down to the lime-quarry: he come here after the war, World War Two, that is, was in the Free French Navy and blown up three times. Now he works the rock-crusher and is making a scandal with the Postmaster's wife. Still, as I said, a man has to have his pleasure, don't he?

Me? It ain't that I'm too old, but it's too much trouble. Me and Lou has got a comfortable arrangement here. Bring some stranger woman into the house, there'd be nothing but trouble. Saw some pretty young chippies down to Florida. But they couldn't see me.

Have a nip of this. Cherry brandy, make it myself. There's the two trees, back of the house. Got a still back of the barn. Chokes you up, first nip? Always does that to folks, first time. Never

expect it to have such a kick. Sure, a still's illegal. But that don't
stop nobody having one. Best thing ever happened to Afton
County was Prohibition. All the Italians had stills anyhow, so
then they made lots of *grappa*, sold it for good prices. Everybody
got their houses painted and got shoes onto their kids' feet and
coats on their backs. The barber even made enough to buy the
old Hebberd place. And he's got five thousand dollars in his
mattress besides. So now, see, a wop Yankee's got the show
place of the village. Makes us all laugh, that does. All except the
Hebberds. Storekeeper's daughter, she that's Storekeeper herself
now, even ran a speak-easy over to State Line. Now *she's* got
more'n anybody, right in the bank. Ayeh, it was Prohibition
ended our depression in these parts.

The still? Back here a ways, in this shed. Skirt this manure pile
where I grow my pumpkins. Mind your head. All copper, see.
Handsome? Never thought of that: know it makes good stuff,
though. All hand driven, no machine to break down. Ain't working it now. That's for fall, after the crops are in. Then winter's
for fixing. Repair your harness, if you still got a team. Oil up
your pump, strip down your thresher or maybe just your lawn-
mower. Cane your busted chair-seats... This here's Blackie's stall.
And his pasture's other side of the gate. Out here. Mind your
head. Here's Blackie now, hanging over the gate. Always comes
when he hears my voice. Lou thinks he just comes for his feed,
but tain't so. Comes for me. Blackie boy, good boy. Feel how
soft his muzzle is. Fine young Black Angus, ain't he? Always get
me a Black Angus. Tastes good all winter.

Shock you? *Soft*. City folks all soft. Get your meat in a store-
package, don't think nothing of it, do you now? Don't know
somebody raised it, fed it, mucked out its stall, and *et* it because
him and his family was hungry and had these damn long winters
to live through.

Go back to Florida in the winter? Not me. Sure winters are
long. Dark and long and hard to live through. —Emmet gets

real low in his spirits, even had to be sent away, one winter, so
as he wouldn't do hisself in.— But it's like this, see. You live off
what you make and what you grow. You work from dawn to dark
and more, to get your independence, but then you're no man's
clock-puncher. You live with the time of year and the time of
day. Sure it's nice to have a light or a stove you can turn on
with a switch or water that comes when you turn on a tap. But
a man can live without these things if he has to. Better live
without, than be a slave to a time-clock or a conveyor-belt. Too
bad I don't know fancy words for explaining my meaning.

Spring comes slow, slush and mud, till one day your hand feels
a clod of soil that shows it's ready for planting. Then ploughing,
then sowing. Summer comes fast, you harvest, you eat good, then
it goes quick. Fall comes, leaves turn and fall down. Trees are
all bare, then snow comes and buries your fields. Emmet gets
down-hearted. You get up in the dark for the milking. Winter
goes on, you think it'll never be over. You wonder why you stay
in the god damn place. But one day you get up, it ain't dark,
sun's got a little bit of warmth, crust on the snow starts melting,
you see the corms on the branches of the swamp-willow trees
is starting to swell up. Sap's running, in you too, and spring's
on the way. Then you know the year's begun again.

9. THE LAND-OWNER

AMBROSE LONGYEAR

It's like this. When those spendthrifts in Washington decided that Springfield needed more water-supply, they and the crooked foreigners that run this Commonwealth decided to rob it from up here in our mountains. There's a lake and there is, or was, a fine fertile valley — about the only one hereabouts that wasn't full of rocks — the other side of Mount Greystone. So they put their dam there.

Flooded the village of West Melville along with the valley. Plopped the people in it into the different villages and townships round the County. We got some here, mostly in that trailer-court down the road. Shiftless bunch, send their kids to our school, go on that welfare themselves, all they're good for is raising our taxes.

Well, that was the live people, the quick, as the Good Book says. But what about the dead? Stands to reason they wouldn't just leave them under water over there. But why should *we* have 'em? That's the question I put at the Town Meeting. Put it right smack to them: what're *we* supposed to do with them? We've got enough of our own. Fact is, too many. We had two grave-yards here already: one behind our Church, just down-street from my place here, and another cross-mountain by the meeting-house that ain't there any more. Some folks once broke away from our church, that was in my grandfather's time, and started their own meeting-house on some Dwiggins land, over there on the back road to State Line. Had to toil up-mountain to get there, carts and carriages used to get stuck in mud or snow. Quite a sight, that must've been. But the Good Lord took matters into his own hands and that meeting-house was struck by lightning one summer. Burnt right to the ground. But the graveyard's still there. The dead have to be respected, whatever their sins were when they were alive. Graves have to be tended. Do you know

36

how much it costs to tend one grave per annum? A pretty penny, I can tell you. And that all goes onto our taxes. Besides which, anybody who amounts to anything has got his own family plot: upkeep has to be paid, every year, out of a man's own pocket.

Well, yes, of course there's that other one, those Catholics call it a cemetery. It's bigger than ours, those foreigners spawn like fish, and it too has to be paid for out of tax-money. Though why that should be I'll never know, as they're not of our faith. As I've said right out in Town Meetings many a time. (A few home-truths are good for the soul.) When I used to go to 'em, that is.

But to get back to the point. What're *we* supposed to do with West Melville's dead? — When? Well, I'd say that was about twenty years ago, my father was still living then, but bed-ridden, so I went to that meeting to represent the whole family. — Now, would you believe it, Lucius Hebberd, Lucius Senior that is, always the closest man in town till then, he spoke right up and said he'd donate his northeast field, free and clear and in perpetuity, for the dead of West Melville. Nobody said a word: struck dumb, I've no doubt. — Something must have been wrong with that field, I always thought. — Well, *I* spoke up, but nobody heeded me. So that's how we got the West Melville graveyard put here in Stonecrop, using *our* tax-money for its upkeep.

But that's not the worst of it. You see, it so happened that Hebberd's northeast field abutted onto the west boundary of the town graveyard. There's an old dry-wall bounds it. Not in good repair now, but 'twould take a lot of work to fix it. And the Hebberds claim that the wall is on church property, so they don't have to keep it up. But that still ain't the whole story. It also happens that the Longyear plot in that graveyard is next to the wall of that field. Always was, time out of mind. When the dead from West Melville was brought here, some of their relations come and planted trees in that Hebberd field. Weeping willows, mostly. Now a willow is a pretty fast-growing tree. You take a fir, now: it'll take a man's whole lifetime for it to get its growth. But a willow's a different matter entirely, grows three, four feet a year. And it's a *trashy* tree — throws its twigs and pods

and suckers off along with its leaves, sheds its trash all over the
place. And a *weeping* willow's the worst. Besides its trash, it's
got all those branches hanging down and spreading out all over.
Believe me, a willow's no respecter of boundaries.

So of course it weren't long before that willow, planted on Hebberd land, began growing over onto the Longyear plot in the
town graveyard, spreading its branches over the monuments
and its trash all over the graves.

But the law is complicated. Makes more money for the lawyers
that way. Issue seems straightforward enough, don't it? Tree
on Hebberd land trespassing on *my* land. For 'tis my land, as
that plot is paid for, year by year, by a Trust Fund. Were that
willow some Hebberd trespassing on one of my fields, I'd have
every right to shoot him. That's the law.

But Hebberds say they deeded the land to the West Melville
dead, so it ain't theirs no more. State says West Melville don't
exist now, so it ain't theirs neither. So whose is it? *I* say if it's
nobody's, then I'll go chop that tree down. Hebberd says if I do
he'll get me jailed. But if it ain't his, what does he care? Pure
spite, wouldn't you say?

Of *course* he's my cousin — we had the same grandparents on
my mother's side. What's that got to do with it?

No, I don't know how it stands at the moment. It's time to plant
corn now. When the days draw in, it's time for haying. Winter,
that's the time for lawing.

There's that good-for-nothing farmer Kroll's son. Back from his
noon-day dinner. Ten minutes late, too. In my day, they didn't
go home to dinner, and if any man was late, he got laid off.
What's the world coming to?

10. THE WIDOW WHO HAD TO STAY

ABIGAIL HEBBERD DWIGGINS

You have to stamp three times on the porch for me to know anyone's there. That's the only way I can hear it. I feel the vibrations through the floor. Emmet McSorley scraped these floors, took seven coats of paint off these wide boards and found this fine pegged oak underneath. Handsome, aren't they? He was the first one in New England to think of doing that. You may think he's just a poor carpenter living down in the Hollow, but he's a man of many talents. That's how we became friends, you know, which we are to this day.

I've sold off most of the old furniture. It was Emmet, in fact, who told me how highly it's regarded in some quarters, which meant it could bring high prices. So the only old things left now are these floors and the stone fireplace and bake-oven, the old lights in the windows — and the house itself, of course. Some find it pretty, and lots want to buy it now because there aren't many of this so-called salt-box style in Afton County. But even if it were ugly, no doubt real estate agents would be after it anyway, just because it was built in 1772! They have no idea how the cold air settles around your feet in winter and sets your bones aching to such a degree that you can count every one of them, more than you'd think a human body could contain.

Quaint, they call it, that you have to tote water from the well in the cellar, go outside to the privy in any weather, clean oil lamps every morning. Or some say, "It's unspoiled." They don't have to live in it.

If you want to ask me a question, young man, you write it down on this pad of paper. Emmet McSorley's the only one whose words I can understand, even after he'd nagged me into taking that course in lip reading...

39

No. I *don't* want to live in this house, I never wanted it in the first place. But when I tried to sell it, there was no market for it, and now it's too late. Where else, now, could I live? I sold that flat pasture to the Weaver, where you see that good-looking modern house over there. I'd sell off more, up-mountain, if I could, but it's too wild up there for most city people. At night there's the bark of a fox or the hoot of an owl, and in some seasons, strange lights raying up from the earth, of which no one knows the cause. It may be some valuable mineral — but I'll never allow any quarrying here, I assure you. The Weaver and Gretchen, his wife, like the life of the woods, but most city people would get lonely and fearful. So I rent out the two southern fields to Kroll for his haying, and sometimes sell off some of my timber. That keeps me going, that and my pension.

When I tried to sell this house, it was after my father had died and my husband and I came back here to take care of my mother. But at that time, before the Music Festival was established or any summer people were looking for dwellings, this township was the poorest of the poor and a *real* backwoods, so there was nobody to buy it. My plan then was to keep back some of my woods for walking around in — for that has always been my enjoyment — and one of my fields; with the money from selling this house, I'd have bought me a trailer, weather-tight and with inside plumbing, and set it up there. They were new-fangled things then and would surely have set Stonecrop by the ears and confirmed their opinion of my character.

You have a question? Well, I was never a house-wife nor did I fit into any of the Stonecrop patterns. Whilst other girls were learning the female arts which would later enslave them, I was away at college. I'm the only female in these parts of my age, or even a lot younger, who had that opportunity. How my father was ever persuaded to do this is still an amazement. It was my mother's doing really, and the only time she ever stood up to him, as she didn't want me chained to the preserve-kettle and the baking-oven, the water-toting and fire-building, and the endless child-bearing — whether a woman was willing or no.

When I'd graduated I came back to a place where I couldn't fit in nor was there anybody would want to marry me. That was all right with me, but time hung heavy. And purses, in our branch of the Hebberd family, were lean. So I took a few more studies in Albany and got my teaching certificate. I got me a post right here in Stonecrop, taught the six-to-nine year-olds right in the little school-house down there in the Hollow. I taught them the usual courses required at the time, their sums and some geography and so on, which bored them as much as it did me, but mostly I read to them and set them to drawing and painting. You'd be surprised what a spark there was in them. It was only the backwardness of their lives, not of their minds, that had stunted their imaginations. The spark was dowsed by the ignorance of parents, who lived in a cultural darkness and wanted everybody else to be in it with them; and by the terrible, hard work that began for almost every child, in those days, before he was even fifteen years old...

Well, my new profession suited me fine as far as work went, but I was otherwise lonely, as can be imagined. Till Cornelius Silvernail — grandfather of young Cornie, who's village police officer now — grew senile and had to retire. There being nobody local to take his place, Ephraim Dwiggins was brought over from Columbia County. His family had lived here at one time; in fact, an Elijah Dwiggins was one of the first twelve settlers that broke away from Afton and founded this benighted village. The reason for that break was not a matter of religious freedom, as some like to think, but the result of a land dispute. Indeed, a more usual reason, with our Yankee forefathers, than religion ever was!

But that's ancient history. Ephraim Dwiggins was born and raised in New York State, and when he came here to work he was regarded as a foreigner. Just as much as if he'd been born in Italy or Ireland... As I was considered much the same, for the reasons I've already told you about, we at once felt a mutual attraction. We taught side by side, though, in the little school house, for two years before we married. You see, we each had a dream, but it took that long to get around to sharing it. New England

reticence, that's called. Both of us liked helping the youngsters,
but what each of us would have liked better was a free life,
with a little fun and adventure in it, and that shared with a mate.
As soon as we found out about each other, Eph bought a motor-
cycle and we got married in the Afton Courthouse. Then we
sped up-mountain with me on the pillion and spent our wedding-
night under the stars. — Luckily it was June and our spot was
free of poison ivy. — Eph called the cycle his white charger
(though Ambie Longyear and others called it the devil's mon-
ster), and we viewed the whole country from it that summer.
We also spent many days picking wild strawberries, hunting
blueberries and fishing for trout in an old punt we fixed up. We
didn't even live in a house, but in a tent on that field yonder.
My father cursed me and Eph, and the tent too, before he died,
but mother did not seem displeased. But by all others, I was considered the disgrace of the County. Why wasn't I in a kitchen,
baking bread and preserving for winter? Well, winter came. It
got cold in the tent, so we got on our white steed and went south.
We saw many cities, many landscapes, and many different kinds
of people, and ended up in a cabin on the Alabama shore. We
had the Gulf for our front yard, and that's where we got our
food. Eph had had a little land left him in Columbia County
which we'd sold, planning to live as we willed till our funds
ran out. But long before that, Mama took sick and we had to
come back. We lived right here. There weren't any jobs, none
at all, half the town was on relief. You'd think it would have
been hardest on Eph — with his quick mind and his wide interests, and his love of roving the earth. But he settled in here, fixed
the place up, planted that rose-garden out back that's all choked
up now, and learned a lot of new things. There were still some
Indians around here then: those that hadn't been killed off by
bloodthirsty Puritans lived on the other side of Greystone Mountain till my land-hungry ancestors pushed them off. Eph learned
their crafts, mostly basket-weaving, and then he started a school,
a kindergarten it would be called now, for the Italian quarry-
workers' children. Taught them English, and those handcrafts.
It was I who couldn't settle down. I felt hemmed in by everything I'd always wanted to get away from. "When are we going

to get away from here, Eph?" I'd ask him, and he'd say, "As soon as your mother gets better." But he knew she wasn't going to get better... All the Hebberds and Longyears gave us the cold shoulder, and laughed behind my back. "Now she can find out what work is," they'd say, or "Now she knows where a woman's place is." The women were the worst: what they couldn't get in the way of freedom for themselves, they didn't want any other woman to have either. In most ways, though, I didn't care what their attitude was, as I always despised these mean-minded, intolerant Yankees, with their Puritan hypocrisy.

You have a question? Well, for them it's go to church on Sunday and cheat the immigrants the rest of the week. Tell their children they're sinners — then take their own dirty little sins, the men that is, over to Hudson on a Saturday night... They don't even admit to themselves how they made their fortunes off the backs of the dispossessed tenant farmers and the Italian poor.

I learned these things at first hand. How that came about was in this way: the War started and Eph volunteered for the Army. Many of the men here were drafted and others went away to work in defense plants. So then there *were* a few jobs, even for women. The limestone quarry started working in earnest, year-round and, when the weather allowed, two shifts. I got me the job there of timekeeper. The workers, you see, were too old for the draft. But that work is so terrible it's like a war itself... So why were these men working there at all, why hadn't they been pensioned off long before? A great many questions arose in my mind while I worked there, matters that neither Eph nor I had ever given a thought to. I realized that, for all my college degree, I was greatly uneducated, and I had no idea how to set about remedying this. There was little or nothing of help in the Afton Library. And that was as far afield as I could go at the time, being tied down by my job on the one hand and caring for Mama on the other. But two years after Eph was sent overseas, she died. The end of ten years of miserable suffering could be no cause for tears. One could only feel relief — for her, and perhaps for me as well. At the funeral — an archaic ritual! — my dry eyes were noted with the usual disapproval. I shed my tears in the solitude of the woods, tears of regret for what her life might have been...

I left here at once, job, house and all — and went straight to New York. There, it didn't take me long to find what I wanted. I attended the Jefferson School for over a year, and also took training in union organizing. My intention was to come back here and start unionizing the quarry-workers. For a start. There was a fine young man at the school, name of Paul Endicott, a school teacher himself by profession, who was going to come here with me and help me.

But "the plans of mice and men," you know. Eph was wounded and sent home. His left leg had been hit by a shell. For a long time he couldn't walk. But after long months of therapy from the hospital in Albany, he could get about again. All those months he cursed at his wound and his crippled life, and had no other thoughts at all. But when he could walk again, soon without even a cane, I was sure his spirits, too, would be cured — and felt sure what could do it. I told him my plan: that we would work together. Just as he'd organized that kindergarten years before, now we could organize a political club to educate the workers here in the County. I had all my books and it wouldn't have taken him long to catch up with me and maybe surpass me.

But something had crippled him up inside, too. He refused to take any interest, even to read. He lived on self-pity. He said it hurt him to walk, and that folks laughed at him when he limped. He took to his bed. When I tried to rouse him by telling him what I had learned, he cursed me. He began to hate me. That's when I began to go deaf. I didn't need that doctor to tell me it was psychosomatic — "it's all in your mind," was his quaint phrase — but that didn't cure me. In spite of everything, though, I started my Political Action Club. Then there was action indeed! But it wasn't political: it was against me. Communist was the least they called me, and some Italian-Americans burnt a cross on our lawn one night. Eph laughed. I bless fate that I couldn't hear his ranting against me, but I did hear him laugh...

For the next five years we lived in a brutal way: silence for me, raging from him, and in complete isolation. As irony would have it, Paul Endicott did come up here, to teach in the new High School. But it was too late by then — for our plans, and for me, too. Those five years, Eph's last, passed as slowly as a century, till the night he died... No one really knew what he died of: he simply wasted away.

Now? Well, I have my friendships — with Emmet McSorley and with my young grand-nephew, Luke Hebberd. And my writing. No, I never show it to anybody but Emmet. And my walks in my patch of woods. The Three Misfits, they call us here! Luke may depend on me for the only understanding he gets, but he's learning to live his own life, in his own way. As for Emmet, the self-taught historian in carpenter's overalls, he's a great man who's wasted his life. And me...well, you can't describe yourself, can you?

I try not to think of my own wasted life, or those terrible years. But sometimes, especially when house-bound by winter, I can't avoid it. I remember the days before Eph and I had to come back here: our joy and our love was then like the fiery heart of a ruby.

What happened? What became of the fire, the juice of life and the joy of living that we had in us?

AFTON COUNTY IMPROVEMENT SOCIETY
in re: Subject of July Meeting

(1) The Dwiggins residence on Main Street just east of Maple is, for the Stonecrop area, a fairly good example of restoration. The house, designed in classic Colonial style of clapboards with four square, wooden pillars supporting the pediment above the second story, was built in 1771, nine years before the (then) Coach House Inn. The land was cleared and the dwelling and its out-buildings were erected by Elijah Dwiggins, one of the first twelve settlers of West Afton which, as we all know, was the former name of Stonecrop. The house was kept in good repair and many improvements were made, including the planting of several wine-glass elms around the extensive grounds, during the ensuing century.

At the time of the Civil War, however, the descendants of Elijah Dwiggins having made unwise investments in out-State enterprises, the then head of the family was forced to sell off all his adjoining fields and his more distant timberlands, and the house began to fall into disrepair. At the same time the sons of that owner, having joined the Union Forces, both lost their lives in the Civil War. Of this rather large family, then, there remained only the householder and his wife, one widowed daughter-in-law and one male grandchild. Of the estate, only the house and grounds remained. The elder Dwigginses having passed away, taxes could no longer be paid, and the property was seized by the Township; the house was sold at auction at the Afton County Court House on July 5, 1867, at noonday. The young Widow Dwiggins, with her male child, removed to New York State, and no member of this family was again a resident of the Township until Ephraim Dwiggins (1905-1951) returned to the Township to take the place, at the time of the latter's retirement, of Cornelius Silvernail the Elder, as Schoolmaster of the Mill Hollow schoolhouse.

The Dwiggins dwelling, meanwhile, was purchased by an immigrant, one "Artie" Handlichek, who was unable to restore it and allowed this fine example of Colonial architecture to go to wrack and ruin. Later, however — in 1930 or thereabouts — another immigrant, namely, Karel Bartushek, purchased the derelict house, and restored its roof. The house is now owned by Karel Bartushek's son, the Postmaster of Stonecrop, who has completely restored grounds, dwelling and out-buildings in a surprisingly tasteful manner. The careful restoration and pleasant appearance of the old Dwiggins place is in stark contrast to

(2) *the former Cobday house* at the southerly section of the Township known as Cobday's Corners. Unlike the former Silvernail place on adjacent land fronting the Mill Hollow Road, which was purchased and restored by Anton Jensen, a member of the Festival Symphony Orchestra, in 1948, the Cobday property was also seized for back taxes, but was never bought by anyone, nor have the Selectmen of the Township ever done anything about its upkeep. Originally a fine example of "Greek Revival" style, this house now lies in ruins. After the roof caved in, the chimney then fell and crashed through the floors of the second and first stories. Now only a part of the south wall of the house remains, rising jaggedly above the ground-level débris of what was once the rest of the dwelling. The building is, of course, impossible to restore. It is now both an eyesore and a hazard for curious children. As Stonecrop Township sees fit to do nothing about this blot on the fair name (as well as on the landscape) of Afton County, it is suggested that our next meeting be devoted to discussion of ways and means of having these ruins removed and replaced by a small park or roadside picnic area, with a suitable plaque erected at one corner, commemorating this lost mansion and its original owner.

Respectfully,
R. *Apthorpe-Jones, III, Sec'y*

11. THE LAD WHO WENT AWAY

ALOYSIUS HALLORAN

Is it ever you've been in New York City? Ever in Pennsy
Station even? Well I'll be telling you, lots of village
lads from about the County left the land and went to the city.
The farms that their folk had were running out. Mine never had
any land to begin with. Me da left the old country during the
potato famine. Came to these rocky hills to better himself
and feed his children. But it wasn't that different. All
he ever got was a shack with a leaky roof and plenty of
cold through the chinks in the winter. Down there by the
swamp, where the trailer-court is now, next to the Dump.
He worked at one thing, then another, then became a plough-
man for old man Longyear. Always walked to work, snow rain
or hot sun. Even if there wasn't no work. Then he'd walk
to Afton, cardboard in his boots, and scavenge. This
shack I'm ending me days in, here on Maple Street, isn't
much different from that one I set up a howl in at me
first peep at this vale o' tears. The town lets me live
in this one, you see — and be sure that nobody'd give 'em
a penny for the rent of it — for the wee-bit work I do
with me shovel in winter and me broom in the summer.

Mosquito-field, that's what we called our swamp-site, and
surely it was as much like a Dump then as now. But the
Yankees were calling it Micktown or Bohunktown, depending
on whichever folk they were wanting to heap their scorn on
that season. Because our kin come here later than theirs
did. And Mick they always called me, even me butties at
the school-house, even the lads I finally run off with.
They could never get their clumsy tongue-clappers round
me name, do you see. Me da said it right, Al-oh-*ay*-shus,
with a fine lilt to it. He died young; walking to the
fields and ploughing them in the rain, he caught the
pneumonia and perished of it.

48

Too many then under our roof. So me and me two butties run
off to the city. When we were lads, do you see, we'd watch
for the train to come through: the driver'd blow the whistle
of his great pow'rful engine and the fireman would stoke
up till the sparks flew from the stack. A fine life we
thought it'd be on the railroads and be making our fortune the whiles, and maybe come back here driving big
cars and handing out a seegar or two, and taking our
mums' hands out o' the washtubs and dressing their tired
selves up in silks. Ochone, windy boys with their heads
in the clouds and their feet in clodhoppers.

It's the lonesomest place the world over, that city. And
the silver that lined your pockets far better'n chopping
corn up here in the Fall, that was soon spent, gone on
the rent of the lonely small room, the greasy meal in the
diner, and an evening or two in the pub with your mates.
All of us lads were after coming back to the village,
but 'twas always "next year" when we saved up a few dollars.
Och, I'm remembering it well, those nights in the city while
I worked as a porter in the big railroad station.

I hear it's tore down now, but in those days there was a
place there much like a tunnel, you could walk up the
in*cline* and look through an arch. There was the street,
all cobbled 'twas then, and up above was the sky. On a
wet night the lights glowed like pools off the cobbles.
On a fine night you could look up and there see the stars.
Glory be to God, there's the church bell tolling six,
another day done.

12. THE DAILY HELP

AMENIA LONGYEAR

No, I'm not bound anyplace. Had thought I'd go cross-lots and tell that Mr. Stone he should think twice before he hires Obediah Lapidus. But when I got as far as this bridge here, I recollected how I don't *know* that Mr. Stone, and furthermore got no business interfering with his plans, or talking against my own neighbor. No, I don't mind having a chat about the old days here, not that I know all that much. But come along back to the cottage and set a while on the porch. It's only a step down the road. Here, opposite the old school-house.

This cottage was built in 1745 but didn't come to the Longyear family till my mother married old Mr. Ambrose's young brother. 'Twas her second matrimonial vow, and I was the only child of it. When Papa died, he willed this house to her, and so when she passed on, it come to me, lock stock and barrel, and nobody ever could take it away from me. Of course, when my time comes, I suppose it'll get sold up to some city folks, just like that old Codwise place got sold to Mr. Stone. He's got big plans for that house, says he's going to restore the central chimney, but it never had none, just an old stove-hole with an old tin flue stickin' out the back.

What was I going to tell that rich city man? Well, nothing much. I only would've said: Obediah Lapidus is *tricky*. When I see him, I say good morning or good evening, as the case may be, because Obediah, he's my *neighbor*, but that's all I ever have to do with him, on account of he's tricky.

The occasion arises — to greet him, I mean — often enough, as I walk every day from my house, here in the Hollow, up to the Corners to the big *house* that used to belong to the old Toupences and now belongs to the people from out-State. I go there mornings, summer and winter, rain or shine, to wash their dishes

50

and make their beds and clean their rooms. Wouldn't you think folks'd have more pride than to hire other folks to clean up their dirt? — But that's neither here nor there.

About Obediah Lapidus: it was like this. I was working over to Melville in the paper mill, before it closed down. (I didn't always have to go out as a daily help, you see.) And I had me this dog. He was a beauty, a great big German shepherd with a fine glossy coat and big brown eyes, and a gentler disposition than many humans I could mention. I told Mama never to let him out whilst I was gone, as I didn't want him to go roving or maybe get hurt. "Mama," I'd tell her every morning as I set out — I had me a car in them days — "don't let the dog out." But one day she forgot, or just didn't think it mattered — I never found out the right of that — and she let him out. Now, he was a good tractable creature, as I've said, but he fell into bad company. There was another dog, a big black one, a-roving the road and the railway tracks, and hunting. My dog fell in with him, and as bad luck would have it, they were robbing Obediah's chicken-house just about dusk, his time for home-coming.

That was long after he'd had to leave this house, and had married that foreign woman, and built him his own place, complete with chicken-house, goat-stall, and, may I say, dung-heap. — Why, didn't anyone tell you yet that Mama was Obediah's stepmother? That's what all the lawsuit was about, after she died. — Anyhow, as you may have noticed, Obediah never goes anyplace, to any job or the like, without his shot-gun in the back of that old car of his. He's done that ever since the depression days, still shoots him a rabbit for his supper, or a woodchuck for the bounty. So, that evening he got home, and there were those two dogs robbing his hen-house. That other dog was smart, he took off, no doubt, quick as a flash. But my dog was a poor dumb innocent. Obediah Lapidus took out his shot-gun and killed my dog. Yes, he killed my dog and put him on my front lawn.

Now do you see why I think he's *tricky?*

All I can say is, lucky he didn't find his *wife* in that hen-house. Sometimes you even have to feel sorry for that woman.

13. THE CARPENTER

EMMET McSORLEY

Why don't you come and set a spell with me? I heard from Abigail that there was a young fellow in the neighborhood, aiming to write a book about the County, and I was hoping you'd pay me a visit. We'll sit here on the porch, if the mosquitoes don't become too irksome: it's a close night. Where are you staying? Afton? That's a step too far from Stonecrop, isn't it? Why don't you stay up the road — the Postmaster's wife rents out rooms in the summer, gets the overflow from the Music Festival, and so does the young barber. Said they hadn't any? Not surprising. They'd be afraid you might write down something to their discredit, and in any case they almost equate writing with black magic. Or the evil eye. Did you note that Angelo Sabato wears garlic around his neck? That's to ward off the *mal òcchio*. There's plenty of ancient superstitions still in existence here. Some of our Irish contingent have a green Easter out in the woods, so the church is half empty that day, and the priest can stretch his lungs, thundering against it. Good exercise for him. Little Silvestro (though he's far from little by now), the hunter who lives up-mountain, could tell you about that. He lived with me for a short time when he was a boy. You might tell him I sent you. I don't see any harm in those old things — there's plenty of worse practices.

As for your going back and forth each day, that seems impractical to me. You're welcome to bed down here for the season, provided you can stand the mess. I'm not much of a housekeeper, and the place has got more cluttered since I started to buy up old glass and china at the auctions and eke out my pension somewhat by selling it. On the other hand, I'd be willing to oblige with such knowledge as I have of the history of Afton County. Or, as you say, its present state and condition.

Provided it's not mere gossip. There's all too much of that in our backwoods, a practice which makes for much meanness and misery.

Why it's still such a backwoods, while so much of the rest of the country grows more and more affluent, and Europe or Asia's a day's flight away, is something I've given some thought to. Of course, it *is* a backwoods, in a geographical sense. But also in a historical one. Melville, now, is on the Hoosac River, plenty of water-power to run those grim Victorian factories — the "dark satanic mills" — over there, and it's on the main Boston-Albany Railroad line. Our river's nothing but a creek in comparison, the only industry it could ever serve was the marble quarry. This plain, small house was put up for the time-keeper, which was my father's job at one point. But the marble began to run out and the quarry was closed entirely after the disaster. (The lime-quarrying wasn't started until some time later, and never has amounted to much in any case.) So after that, the immigrants who were brought here, in the first flush of the discovery of mineral and rock, to quarry and mine and smelt it, were too poor to go anywhere else, just had to stay here and become poorer — and *rot*. Work makes man, some believe. Whether or no, the opposite is surely true: being out of work unmakes men, and leads to apathy and spiritual decay. The landowners who brought the workers here had their own kind of decay: felt no responsibility for those who'd come and then been stranded.

The County was first settled, however, for the very reason that it *was* a backwoods. At one time — seems long ago now — the most important commodity in New England was freedom. Perhaps not the same sort of freedom we might seek after now, but it *was* that, nevertheless. Freedom to worship in the way one wanted, to have land to till, a representative government, and breathing-space all around. To grow in one's own way. A type of fierce individualism that no longer exists. And with it, a sense of responsibility towards others. However narrow they were — and, yes, they were narrow and intolerant — those early settlers had *spirit*. But the ones who broke away first from Hartford or Boston to Afton, then from Afton to here, picked themselves a dark pocket. Of course the mountains are beautiful, whether covered in greenery as now, or sheer white with snow in the winter — and most of all, in June with a great burst of mountain laurel. That glory can equal, in its season, what can be gained from a city's museums or libraries. But these mountains also hem us in on all sides. Preclude growth and mingling. By the same token, have filled the arable land with rocks. All these picturesque old dry walls around there were hauled from the earth by the groans of men's backs. Wasn't really suitable land for farming and dairying.

It wasn't only the poor Italians that cleared the fields, either. That old wall between my house and the river, for instance, where I first saw you sitting, this sundown — do you know who built it? Like many another, 'twas built by black men. You'll hear the tale told of the underground railway that had its "station" in Stonecrop. True enough, but what became of the slaves, once they'd escaped? It was they who freed much of this soil of its rocks, built the walls, excavated the foundations for the grand houses of Dwigginses, Hebberds and Longyears... No, there's none left here now, nor is their history written in books.

The most interesting part of living, life-long, in a small town is that you can see the whole history of our country laid out before your eyes, in what you might call microcosm. By what's happened to the land, the houses, the descendents of those who first came to it. And by what the younger ones want out of life today.

Och, these midges are getting pesky. Or maybe it's just their turn to be out. Time for us to go indoors, light the lamp, and have us a little liquid refreshment.

Just move that box of old glass off that Shaker rocker and sit you down, and I'll set aside these books on the table. Found me a fine batch today on early settlements around Greystone, and some interesting poetry too. Found 'em in an old barn in Afton.

Now, whom have you talked to so far? Obediah Lapidus? Him and some kind of scandal? Why, lad, I wouldn't soil my mouth with it, were it one. But it was no scandal. It was scandalous behavior on the part of the narrow, bigoted people around him, though perhaps that only due to their lack of education. What Obediah did was only what this country was supposedly founded for, or one of the reasons.

You know how most men just plod through their lives, never do a thing out of the way, makes you wonder how we ever got down out of the trees and stood upright in the first place? — but then one of them will do one thing, one fine thing, totally unexpected? What Obediah did was marry the oldest Ghitalla girl. A Protestant Yankee met up with an Italian Catholic, descendent of old settler with offspring of immigrant. It was a love-match. Oh, there's been a-plenty of old settlers' sons sowed their wild oats with young Italian girls, sowed their seed you might say, but never married them. It was the marriage that made the scandal! Ironic, isn't it? Each sect thinks it owns Christ, and everybody else is a heretic. I guess if the poetess whose words are inscribed on the Statue of Liberty came up here, she having been a Jewish lady, they'd run her out of town. Even in the Catholic cemetery, the Irish are buried on one side, the Italians on the other. Bigotry's hardly the word.

It must be the long winters here. Folks get to brooding on petty things. And the mountains themselves cutting us off from the rest of the world, we become suspicious of strangers, of each other, or of any unusual event.

Don't get it into your head that Obediah Lapidus was some kind of crusader. He's as bigoted as the rest of them, and as dissatisfied too. Even voted for Wallace — and I don't mean Henry! Yes, lots are dissatisfied. The old-time Yankees because they lost their power, the new ones, immigrants, because they never found their El Dorado. But you must have gleaned that by now.

As for Obediah, he was made more so by being done out of his property. But I'll say this: once he'd lost his lawsuit, he put it all behind him. Doesn't brood on it. Even chops stove-wood for Amenia Longyear every fall — though being such a crusty fellow, Obediah doesn't want anyone to know it — and even though Amenia has a mean tongue always wagging against him. Well, she got property she'd no right to — if you think within that framework, which indeed I do not — so I suppose she has to be on the defensive about it... No, Obediah didn't brood, and that's because he's been happy with his mate these thirty years.

But my, it was terrible when they first married: ostracized, you might say, by both sides. Obediah's uncle Zach — the only other Lapidus left — struck his name out of the family Bible, Obediah couldn't go to church, and he had a hard time getting work. His wife was cast out of *her* church, and even her own father wouldn't speak to her. That's all over long ago, in any active sort of way at least, but it narrowed Obediah's life, by making them keep to themselves. The lawsuit? That's another disagreeable story. I don't know as I've the heart for it, leastways not tonight..

What a lot of terrible things have been done in the name of property! And even more so in the name of religion. Remember what Bernard Shaw said, when specifying his own last rites? No Christian burial, he said, the Cross having become such a symbol of bloodshed and violence. But he recanted in the end, they say. I hope I won't.

Oh, that — I gave up attending Mass in a church a long time ago. I made my worship up-mountain where the laurel blooms. Before I got so stiff in the joints. Now I do a lot more reading. In any case, I've always believed that *"man's the measure"* — but the way things are going in the world, that gets harder to believe every year.

I hope you'll consider staying here. It may not be comfortable, but it will be convenient. And I'd like to show you some of my books. I found one today, poetry by Trumbull Stickney. I've been looking for it ever since I saw just one piece by him that stuck in my mind. I suppose you'd say he was a Victorian, but this one poem says a great deal for today — to me, anyhow. He was born in 1874, not all that long before me — a mere fifteen years or so (perhaps I'm a Victorian too! — though of quite another class, of course), but he didn't live as long as I have into this century of upheavals and wars. Here, take the book along with you — I'll mark the place — and be welcome to it.

"...In the country I remember"

It's autumn in the country I remember.

How warm a wind blew here about the ways!
And shadows on the hillside lay to slumber
During the long sun-sweetened days.

It's cold abroad the country I remember.

The swallows veering skimmed the golden grain
At midday with a wing aslant and limber;
And yellow cattle browsed upon the plain.

It's empty down the country I remember.

I had a sister lovely in my sight:
Her hair was dark, her eyes were very somber;
We sang together in the woods at night.

It's lonely in the country I remember.

The babble of our children fills my ears,
And on our hearth I stare the perished ember
To flames that show all starry thro' my tears.

It's dark about the country I remember.

There are the mountains where I lived. The path
Is slushed with cattle-tracks and fallen timber,
The stumps are twisted by the tempests' wrath.

But that I knew these places are my own,
I'd ask how came such wretchedness to cumber
The earth, and I to people it alone.

It rains across the country I remember.

Trumbull Stickney (1874-1904)

14. THE WEAVER

MAX JOOST

There was a song in an old musical with a line that went "And time stood still..."

In fact I went to that musical, took my girl with me. Not the girl I married, but before that; she was a fellow-student and what we used to call a gorgeous redhead. That's all I remember about her now. I don't remember much about that show, either, except the one line.

And that line certainly isn't true!

I came up here in the Thirties. The Depression. You wouldn't remember, but it's true about people selling apples on street-corners. My father stood in the bread-line. I had to leave school — which was probably good for me, though I didn't think so at the time. I was a talented boy, or thought to be so, and though my people were working-class, I was sent to a special school where all sorts of "special" kids were learning music, painting, theatre arts, and so on, and all of us pretty pleased with ourselves: a bunch of untried and unproven young cubs, in fact.

Well, I came up here, I can't even remember what prompted me, some bit of pure chance, and I'd never seen anything so beautiful. (Never have since, either.) All I knew of "country" till then was a ratty boys' camp in Jersey. I got some odd jobs to do around the Summer Playhouse in Afton. I slept in the barn they used for a workshop at night and painted flats all day long, and got my meals free. Same flats week after week, and ten plays, ten weeks later, were they soggy! Well there were a lot of others like me apprenticed there, young snot-noses that had always had parents to pay for everything and get them out of scrapes and get their teeth straightened and their underwear washed and all that. Winter comes early here, as you've probably heard already;

our clothes weren't warm enough, and the Playhouse had closed for the season. The young ones mostly hightailed it back to the city, but a few stayed. Among them was Gretchen, the scene designer's apprentice, and an aspiring painter. She stayed on because of me, and later, after we were married, because she grew to love this country too. The winter, as I soon discovered — and I've never changed my mind about that — was even more beautiful than the summer. It was also what you might call basic. Survival was the main preoccupation. No more time for bull sessions about how we were going to set the world on fire, or change it, or both. No parental handouts to live on in those days, you see. Just sheer necessity took over.

How did I live? It seemed miraculous at the time: over the other side of Greystone Mountain, outside a little village called Cobbs Crossing there was an artists' and craftsmen's colony. It had been there all along — in fact for about ten years, only we'd never heard of it. The people there kept to themselves, sold their work through a cooperative in Afton. There were several painters there who'd returned from Paris and found Greenwich Vilage not to their taste. Or anywhere in a city. And lots of craftsmen — potters, weavers, cabinet-makers, a typographer, even an old Austrian who made musical instruments. But the main thing, the cornerstone of it you might say, was that it was a cooperative. All the things that are such fads now, ecology, communes, living off the land you live *on*, and so on, were practiced there without ever being given labels. It was started, of course, by one man. He wrote a lot of books about the benefits *to the arts* of collective living — and I've no doubt they'll all be reissued now, and be only half understood by those who buy them... As for me, my good fortune was that this man was a weaver, at one time a famous one, and he took me on as his apprentice and taught me my craft.

My work caught the eye of a New York dress designer. The Depression was over and New York became a glittering, high-fashion place. There were a lot of uses for hand-woven, one-of-a-kind textiles, and high prices were paid for them. Our commune got quite affluent for a while, in fact we built a lot of new, snug studios, and a summer concert hall.

Gretchen, all this time, had been painting away, learning *her* craft, breaking new ground to a certain extent, and selling a lot of her work through our Guild in Afton. But when my stuff caught on she began to object to my turning all the fees over to the community. Even though that was the custom. Maybe she was a little jealous, I don't know... A gallery owner from New York saw her work in Afton, gave her a show and took Gretchen on as one of her, as they revoltingly call it, "stable"... This satisfied Gretchen, at least for then, and eased the tension between us.

Then the war came. The community simply disintegrated. Many members were Objectors. Some went to Canada, some were sent to those internment camps. Others, who had children, got deferred and went off to places like Taos and Carmel where, to this day, they live well on the stuff they make now for tourists... I was deferred, of course, because of my leg.

I see you trying hard not to look at it, or at my limp, but as I've been like this since I was eight years old, it doesn't embarrass *me*, so it needn't you. I'm only pleased that I can get along without a brace, and do as good a day's work as any other man. — In fact, with some help from Foley the stone mason, I built this house. — And glad that kids don't have to get polio any more.

But if I hadn't been deferred, I figured I'd have ended up in one of those camps with some of my friends. I didn't feel comfortable, being deferred like that. So I left here, in 1943 or thereabouts, and joined the Friends Service Committee. There was plenty to do in the Ambulance Corps, even for a man with a limp, and I wound up in France.

When I came back, afterwards, Gretchen had left. She hadn't left *me*, but she'd decided that she had to live in New York for the sake of her career. She came back here for a while, but she no longer liked it. In fact, she hated being here. So we both went to New York. I found us a big airy loft which we could divide up into studios for each of us.

Being in the city changed everything for me. I could no longer raise our food or keep our own roof in repair. There was no more cooperative, where everything was shared. It was each man for himself. — In other words, for the first time in my life, really, I needed *money*. Money for rent, for food, for heat, for Gretchen's paint and canvas. And there was no longer a guild which sold my work. So just when I needed money the most, I had nowhere to make any.

I went to see one of the gals I'd woven fabrics for — the war had just about killed that too, the luxury dress trade. She sent me to see some of the big commercial dress firms. Most of them laughed in my face — "a *weaver* for Christ's sake" — but one of them realized that as I designed all my fabrics myself, I could probably design stuff that was suitable for mass production.

So that's what I did. For twenty years. Twenty years, I can't believe it now! And it was all rubbish. Worse than that. A betrayal of everything I believed in and knew how to do. I keep all the designs over there in those cases. To remind myself.

The ironic part is that Gretchen's health had always been good here. Even the coldest winters were dry, and she never had any trouble with her joints until she went back to New York. It was New York — the damp and the slush, maybe the dirt and discomfort too — that put her in that wheelchair. Where she'll be for the rest of her life.

Her painting? Well, I wouldn't say New York helped her career all that much. She didn't sell any more paintings there on the spot than she had from up here through her gallery. There's a thousand competent, talented painters in New York. But the more she was forced to realize that that's *all* she was, the more ambitious she became, until finally she was just obsessed, eaten up, with all the striving and competitiveness. *That*, you see, had been eliminated from our lives by our community living — that kind of personal ambition that leads to hardness and envy, ego-drive; and what made the old man who started the place so great was that he realized that. It's always been my private thought that Gretchen's condition was brought on by her obsession and then in the end, her bitterness. But I never mention this. Certainly it's no medical fact. And now of course her hands are crippled up too (and she's no Matisse) so she can't paint at all.

Me? What have I got to be bitter about except my own foolishness? And weakness.

It's not Gretchen's fault that *I* was so obsessed with *her* that I let us both do something that, all along, I knew was wrong and would be disastrous.

But I'm sad. Remember what I said a while back, about time? that it *doesn't* stand still? You see, when I went to New York, it was always in the back of my mind that I could come back here any time I wanted. Even though our cooperative was gone. I always felt it was dormant rather than dead. And as the years passed and the economy changed, I saw that the Guild could easily be revived, that there was a market for craftwork such as there'd never been before; as the society changed there were new craftsmen coming along, eager to find a place to live and work in and an outlet for their goods. Why, I even went so far as to come up here ten years ago and buy this piece of land from Abigail Dwiggins. I bought it, yes, but never did anything with it, never in all that time. Why? Same reason as why I'm sad and full of regrets.

I began to enjoy my rotten commercial work. Or rather, I didn't enjoy the *work* (it gave me ulcers, in fact, what a cliché!): I enjoyed the benefits received from it. I got famous and I got rich. I taught at Pratt too, commercial design for God's sake, and had a lot of hero-worshipping pupils: a corruptor of youth, wasn't I? — as well as of myself. We moved out of our loft, bought a house on Twelfth Street, made it over, built two studios. Every time I got another twenty-five or thirty thousand, I'd decide to put it away, use it to come back here. But I never did. I bought things: that house, fine clothes and leather luggage, paintings and art objects and furniture, trips to Europe and five hundred hours with an analyst. "*Next* year I'll give it up and go back to Afton County and my own work. Next year," I told myself. Year after year.

You know who the devil is? He's Mammon. It's the *little* temptations that finally turn a man rotten. I never killed anyone, was never unfaithful to Gretchen in any serious way, never coveted my neighbors' wife, ox, or job. I just let myself get soft.

The reason I mention the devil is because I found, when I came back here, that I really had sold my soul. The creative part of it, do you see? And not for Helen of Troy and great knowledge or anything like that. Just for the admiration of people I didn't even like and for a lot of things, stuff, that I won't even have around the place now.

That's it in the well-known nutshell: I only gave it all up and came back here when Gretchen's doctor said she couldn't live in New York any more. And then, when I got here, my work was no good.

I've revived the Guild, and I run it. Sell other people's work there. Ironic, isn't it? And not a very unusual story, sounds like a sentimental Thomas Wolfe title. Not even interesting enough to bother writing down, I shouldn't think.

Well, there goes Gretchen's bell. It's the time of day I wheel her chair out to the garden when the weather's fine.

15. THE COWHAND

ANEURIN WILLIAMS

Wales was where I was born, and Pennsylvania was where
I grew up. Coal country, both. You could never imagine
how ugly and harsh such places are, 'less you've seen
pictures of them. I recall well our village in the Rhonda.
Everything built of the rocks and stones cast off from
the mineheads. Cottages all in a row, holding each
other up, you might say, stone, stone-cold, no water,
a stinking privy in back, and the black smuts over all.
Up at five in the cold candle-light, my mother's shawl
a piece of worn sacking, and my wee brother swaddled in same.
All us boys went down at age ten or twelve. Up in the dark,
come home in the dark, having been in the dark all the day.
The main color, 'sides the black soot, was blue. Blue
lips and blue fingertips. Besides warmth, we were wanting
our tea. But often enough there wasn't a lump of the coal
we ourselves had mined out, nor more than a slice of bread
each, spread with dripping, or maybe a cold potato.
There wasn't a Union, then, do you see, no Bevan, "Nye"
he was called — just like the nickname I have myself.

Do you ever think about coal? Coal can cost a man's life.
When you stoke up your stove or your hearth, you're not
burning black lumps of carbon, but men's blood and bones.

But that wasn't the worst: after the war, the first one that is,
the mines were closed down and there wasn't yet even the dole.
Miners in bands big as battalions roamed the highways and
byways of England, singing and begging their bread.
Fancy that, the proud singers of Welsh Eis*tedd*fods —
singing for bread.

So then, and how he did that I was too young to know,
my father took us all on a bladdy great boat, and we

went to the coal-mines of Monongahela. Slag-heaps we had
for our landscape. But though house and town were no better,
wages were fairer and we boys got some schooling. I was
always small, do you see, p'raps due to those scant teas
in the Rhonda. You might think me shrunken with age,
but I was always like this, and so, when I was fifteen,
down to the pits, to the smaller crawl-shafts, once again.
My father was smothered by coal-gas one night-shift,
and later one brother was crushed in a cave-in. I felt
like I'd never seen aught but the darkness and grime
of the darkness that lives deep in the earth.
So it was that I left. I wandered the roads, slept
in their jungles with hobos, at last found myself in a
city, Boston it was, the depression nigh over, got me
a job on the docks, married a young Irish girl fresh from
the Emerald Isle as they call it. She was in service,
died young of our still-born child. We'd lived in
tenement streets, all swarming with people their noise
and their refuse. I still felt as I had in the mines.
I'd never seen the sun rise over a green-wooded mountain,
or a deep sky at night filled with stars. So again
I took off, and one summer up here I got me this job,
milked the cows and mucked out their stalls. Now
the dairy business is gone, we've only the one cow left,
but I stay on, I'm useful with horses and tractors
and things that need putting right. I sleep right here
in this stall long-side Brownie. Her manners are gentle,
and the breath from her grass-cud smells sweet.
She gives good milk and she knows my hands. Why should I
mind cleaning her stall? She can't do it herself,
now can she?

Farmer Kroll says why don't you take your pension, old Nye,
and go live in a house in the village? What would I ever do
there? I said back. So here I am, and I wouldn't change
this life for another.

THE COUNTY ARCHIVES

Cornelius Longyear and Joshua Codwise built the COACH-HOUSE INN on the corner of Main and North Maple Streets in 1782, which now houses, in part, the Town Rooms — namely, the Library, the Town "Hall," and other government offices. But when built, it was used as a hotel and post road stopover. It was the first two-story house built in West Afton (now Stonecrop), and history tells us it also housed the first store in town. No doubt this, together with the site previously chosen for the first "Meeting House" had a great bearing on locating the present "Center" of West Afton (now Stonecrop).

Major Cornelius Longyear is known to have been the first merchant in Stonecrop. He first sold dry goods, spices and rum in the Coach-House Inn but later set up the frame building on South Maple Street which, enlarged, stands to this day. He bought out Joshua Codwise, and took his brother-in-law, Nathan Hebberd, as his partner. It was in these two places of business that men would gather to talk over the village politics, relate former experiences and often amuse themselves by playing practical jokes on one another. No person made it their business to furnish amusement for one another, yet they had fun, often boisterous and rude.

Other early merchants were Judson Cobday who had a store where Foley's Masonry now stands, and Zachariah Lapidus the blacksmith who established his smithy behind the Inn in the then disused stables (now torn down). The Shakers produced flour in the Mill behind Maple Street for a few years, before they moved on to Lebanon. Part of the Mill, then derelict, was torn down but the remainder, which now houses the feed of Hebberd's Hardware Store, can be seen to this day beside the bridge which crosses the mill-stream dam.

(At the request of the Afton Rotary Club, Mrs. Anne Bartushek, Librarian of the Stonecrop Public Library, will continue her articles in *The Nickel Saver* during the next three issues.)

NEXT WEEK: *Why the Town of West Melville was flooded.*

16. THE DEACON

LUCIUS HEBBERD, JR.

How are you this fine afternoon? Yes, it's a mite muggy, but it's nice to see the sun. I hear it's ninety-two degrees down to Afton, but it's only eighty-five here. Of course, it's a little colder here in winter, but not enough to matter. I'm told you want to talk about the future of the Township. Yes, I might say a word or two. Just wait till I find Angie Sabato his honing-stone. You know this young fella, do you, Angie? Then you know he won't mind waiting a few minutes while I rummage around for your stone. Mighty particular stone Angie wants, but they're not made any more and, as he only wants one every couple of years, they get shoved around some. Ayeh, here's the box under this nailkeg. No, it *doesn't* sell for two ninety-five. That was three years ago. It now sells for three and a quarter. You have to face the economic facts of life, Angie. Got a good Republican government in the White House now, but even *they* can't put the prices back where they used to be. It's just as hard on the storekeeper as the working man. Maybe more so: can't hardly pay our taxes out of our sales, much less provide for our families. All right, Angie, I'll trust you for the thirty cents.

That Angie, he can take up more time getting his honing-stone than a new summer fellow getting all his garden equipment. And it stands to reason he's got the thirty cents, for there he goes, heading up-street to Dee's store to buy a jug of *vino*, as they call it.

Now, about this Township. Most folks around here don't think it's *got* a future, but I beg to differ. Come along to the back room here and I'll show you my plans. It's slack-time in the store now and anyhow my Dad'll be back from his dinner any minute, as it's gone one o'clock, and he can sell anything from a tenpenny nail to a power-saw. He's a whiz, my Dad, eighty-three years old and still knows the price of everything in this store.

Now, what the Township needs is a shopping center. It doesn't pay to be old-fashioned like Afton. They won't allow any shopping centers there. You can't even build a new *house* there without Zoning Board approval. They want to keep it "unspoiled." It's true they've got a prime Bulfinch church and some fine shade trees on their main street, and all the fine old mansions behind them. But you can't live on those things. Live on the Music Festival? How can you make a year's living out of an eight-week summer season? And what's *in* those fine houses? Rooms to rent to summer tourists, and antiques for sale in the parlour, or else a tea-room. I can tell you, I wouldn't have any tourists tracking through my house or gaping at the family chinaware. And is that any way to live for a grown man? As for that Festival, it's no good to rely on music for your economy. How long do you think people are going to want to go on listening to that highbrow stuff anyhow? Yes, indeedy, I know it's gone on for twenty years, but some fads are longer lasting than others. Take the hardware business. There's no fad about that. And if people want more modern equipment, well, you can see we've put in tractor-mowers and garden furniture and power tools. City folks don't like hand tools, and they like to take their ease outdoors. That is, when it's not raining. No skin off my nose: we supply them with what they want. Then in the winter we've got the fuel and the grain that us natives need. That's why this store's been in business in the same spot for more than a hundred and fifty years. We keep up with the times, always have. Only thing not up-to-date is this perishing old building. Can't modernize *it*. I'll tear it down when we get our shopping center. And the rest of that useless old Shaker mill too, for that's where I aim to put the laundromat. Now see on this table, this is my model of the shopping center. You'll note how there's an *es*planade along the river, all sheltered and shaded like a lath-house, and the stores and services built in a long row facing onto it. Parking in back. With what's there now? There isn't anything there now worth saving. Post Office is out of the way, other side of Maple Street. Best thing to do with those ramshackle places on Main Street is tear them down. Make the room we need that way. Saw me an *es*planade like this when I took my survey, two winters ago, in California. *Muzak* playing in it. Lots of palm trees in big planters.

How's that? Well, in this climate you could grow plastic ones,
of course. Cheaper upkeep, too... Built these models myself, last
winter. Now here's the new hardware store and grain depot, and
the bay for the oil trucks. Then comes a nice café with outside
tables. Woman over to Melville, runs a tea-room there, is going
to take that. Next, a new barber shop *with* ladies' hair-dressing
attached. Next, the Town Hall, a building all to itself, spanking
new and a place for the town to be proud of. Maybe here a de-
partment store — small for a starter, but room to expand. At
the end there, the laundromat, like I said. Here? That's the
grocery store. Dee Borgese can take it or leave it. Her mother's
old place is an eyesore, and nothing to buy in it that modern folks want. If she doesn't want to join in with us, then
I'll get a branch of the First National to come in, and she can
lump it.

We'll have the finest shopping center in the County, and folks
will come from all *over* the County to use it. Then we'll be a
look-alive town again, like we used to be in the ore and marble
days. The town was up-and-coming at that time. But it doesn't
pay to look backward. And my Dad agrees with me one hundred
percent. Only snag is, my brother Marcus *don't*. He's hanging
onto his share of that old mill and impeding progress. Shakers
cleared out of here in 1810. Moved over to Lebanon. Left that
mill abandoned, and we took it for the unpaid taxes. But my
brother's got this bee in his bonnet, wants to restore it, for goodness' sake, and fill it full of that Shaker stuff he and Emmet Mc-
Sorley collect. *I* wouldn't give it house-room.

My life in Stonecrop? We Hebberds aren't much given to talking
about ourselves. We've always lived here, ever since it began
as West Afton: folks know who we are and where we stemmed
from. The first Hebberd house is no longer in the family. We —
my Dad and I and Marcus, and our wives and children — all live
in the 1886 house, the Victorian one on the farm down the State
Road. The second Hebberd house is much older, it's the salt-box
up-mountain from the Hollow, lived in by an elderly relative.
My other sister-in-law and that good-for-nothing son of hers live
on Maple other side of Main Street; they rent from Ambie Longyear.

As for me, I run this store, and happy to do so, and am Vice-President of my Dad's Savings Bank over to Melville. And I'm Deacon of our Church, the Congregational Meeting House on Main Street. You're welcome to attend any Sunday. Hebberds have always been Deacons there, and I'm proud I was chosen.

Well, now. There's Dad busy with that Mr. Stone — he buys a peck of things every time he comes up from the city — and here comes Emmet McSorley, probably wants a few nails. That man uses more nails than you'd believe, even now he's retired. So I'll have to leave you.

Why don't you stay and look at my model a while longer?

17. THE STOREKEEPER'S BROTHER

ANCHISIO VARCONI

What do you think of this village? Did you ever see anything so mean and run-down? I'd like to show you something, and that's what those *re*search guys from Boston wrote down in their Guide Book. That was a WPA project. One of FDR's plans for helping people during the Depression. A lot of artists painted murals in Post Offices (not *this* one, to be sure!), and a lot of starving authors were sent out in all states of the Union to write up the history of each one of them. It wasn't FDR's fault that some of those writers were stuck-up city bastards. The crew that came to Stonecrop went up-street and down asking all of us if we were summer people or natives. "What do you mean by natives?" Emmet McSorley, who was repairing this roof at the time, asked them. "Do you mean 'lesser breeds without the law'?" But they didn't get it. They asked were we Americans of Italian descent. "No," the Old Barber told them. "We're wop-Yankees. That's what we're called and that's what we are." Actually the crew wasn't three guys, but two fellows and one girl, only the girl looked more like a fellow than the fellows did. Dee called her a snotty bitch. Dee learnt to talk tough where she used to work, I guess. One of those guys is rich now — writes pornography for paperbacks. But at the time he was as dumb as the other two.

Mamma was still alive when they came. Mamma was a big woman, tall and upstanding, taller even than I am now, even when she was over seventy and had worked like a slave all her life. — Our family came from Piedmont, *Northern* Italy, so we're tall and lighter complexioned than all these Sicilians and Calabrians around here. — Well, Mamma had a sense of humor, no matter how tough things were. For instance, when some summer person would come in here for the first time and buy a lot of groceries, she'd pretend she couldn't read or add. She kept a little pad of paper and a pencil right here on top of this cash register. She'd hand them

to the customer and say, "You write 'em down and add 'em up."
That way she could tell right off if they were honest or not, see?

Well, that crew from Boston came in here and started question-
ing her. She pretended she couldn't speak English, and that Dee
and me couldn't either, even though we'd just been seen coming
out of the schoolhouse that used to be practically next door!
Oh, they got a fund of misinformation all right! The Old Barber
gave them some, and the Hebberds some more. Old Man Longyear didn't tell them anything, just threw them off his place. So
you won't want to go by that Guide Book.

But it was their own eyes that told them how this town *looks*.
Nobody could fib about that. They must've been near-sighted. Or
maybe they were romantic... This book's pretty dog-eared now
but you can still read it. Here, this is the part:

> "Continuing west from West Melville [which of course is
> under water now], Mass. 49 gradually descends the narrow-
> ing river valley, from where we have a spectacular view of
> the hills, known locally as 'trains,' a phenomenon created
> by the Ice Age, to its source in STONECROP, whose his-
> tory can be read in its buildings. Square white houses, im-
> posing and sheltered behind graceful wineglass elms, and set
> in well-kept gardens, grace the quiet and shady Main Street,
> and silently describe a prosperous nineteenth century. On
> Maple Street stands the interesting Federal-era building which
> houses Hebberd's Feed and Grain Store; below it, beside
> the dam which is near the source of the West Afton River,
> stands the old Shaker Mill (part torn down, and now used
> for storage by Hebberd's). The cottages across from the
> store are relics of the mining and quarrying days which
> created the Township's prosperity and attracted colonies of
> Irish and Italian laborers, whose descendants may be found
> here to this day, assimilated into village life in the way that
> is uniquely American."

I grant you the trees died of the Dutch elm disease, and one
reason the street's so pot-holed and noisy is because the trucks
all pass through on their way to Albany and the Thruway. But

otherwise it's about the same. You can see those famous signs of "prosperity" on Maple Street — that old fellow Halloran lives in one of them, town lets him have it, well, nobody else would take it, no question about that! In fact, you can see those signs right here in this old store. Doesn't sound much like what you see out of this window, does it?

One time there was a meeting of the VFW about what if the Russians dropped an atom bomb on New England. Maybe you remember all that Civilian Defense stuff? When people in Afton were building shelters in their backyards and buying guns to keep other people out of the useless contraptions? — Well, at that time I still used to come up here from Afton, where I've lived and worked ever since I got out of school, to the meetings at my old VFW Post — right down-street in what used to be our school-house. The Director of Civilian Defense from Boston came to speak to us. Factory towns and state capitals were like to get hit first, he said. "So right here in Stonecrop is the *key point*," he told us. Well, we couldn't get that at all. "Oh, yes," he said, "the refugees from Springfield will trek West and those from Albany will trek East, and they'll all converge right here." So he wanted to know how many doctors and nurses we had, and how many extra beds and canned goods and so on. Of course there weren't *any*... So I looked out the window, and then I looked at the city guy, and I raised my hand and said, "When all those people from Albany and Springfield get here and see what Stonecrop looks like, won't they think it's already *been* bombed?" Well, that made everybody mad, not just the guy from Boston, so I didn't come to any more meetings.

Here comes the truck with the Sunday papers. And here comes Dee back from Mass. She'll be in a temper, or I'd ask you to stay. Dee doesn't like to go to Mass, no question about that, but if she didn't it would be a scandal and nobody'd trade in this store. Anyhow, Sundays are the busiest days here. All the summer people want their Sunday *Times* and so we charge seventy-five cents apiece for them. And sell them by the dozens.

Why don't you drop around this evening and have a beer with us?

18. THE SOLITARY WALKER

MARCUS HEBBERD

Come to visit our church, have you? I don't recommend today's service! They call it Laymen's Sunday — that's just a fancy name for raising money. They send the preacher home to his dinner, and the Deacon, my brother Lucius that is, and the three vestrymen, my father and two more of our relatives, sit down at the communion table and discuss the preacher's salary and the general upkeep of the building, and then they gouge all they can out of the congregation. It's always the same dialogue: my father kicks off with, "Now, just what *is* a church?" and then Cousin Tibbs says, "A church is a place of worship," and then my brother Lucius Junior says, "And what does it take to make a place of worship?" And then they all say, in chorus, very distinct and wooden, like in some school play: "*Money*." All the while my poor sister-in-law, the one my other brother deserted, is playing "Abide With Me," very soft, on the wheezy organ. (They don't have to discuss her salary, as she doesn't get any.)

I tell you, it fairly turns my stomach to have that kind of thing going on in a church. Not that I'm a believer; in fact, I'm an atheist, and I wouldn't go at all if it weren't more trouble than it's worth to stay away, but it turns my stomach anyhow. So I always sneak out on Laymen's Sunday and go for one of my walks.

Today I'm going down to Mill Hollow and then walk the tracks up to a place I know beyond the old marble quarry. You've never seen the old quarry? Couldn't find it? Well, I don't mind if you walk a ways with me. We can take your car down to the Hollow if you want. This your car? Got a lot of mileage on it, hasn't it? Just down the Afton Road to the Corners and turn right...

There's that unfortunate woman, Vittoria Stagliano, sitting all alone on her terrace. Foleys, I guess, are at *their* church... And there's Angie Sabato sitting under his tree, honing his scythes.

75

Keeps busy even on a Sunday. I see he knows you. We Hebberds were pretty surprised, after you came, when we heard that these people would talk to you. People hereabouts, whether they're Yankee born or foreigners, are pretty close-mouthed. Except for Emmet McSorley, he loves to chin-wag. Yes, we were surprised, but then I figured folks will talk to a stranger sooner than to a neighbor. Some of them, anyhow. A neighbor's not a very safe person to exchange a confidence with: you never know how it'll get twisted around in the retelling. And lots here are lonely. Not us Hebberds, of course, as we have each other. A close-knit family, people say, and they're right. Anyhow, lots of these folks that talk to you see no harm in it, as they don't believe a young fellow like you is really going to write any book. And even if you did, they'd never read it.

Well, here we are. Park by the bridge, just beyond Emmet's house.

Now we take the tracks, or what's left of them, upstream. I'll point out your turn-off for you. Where I'm going is an old cave about a half-mile above the disused quarry. There are a lot of those old caves around — like the one where that baby who's called, now, Silvestro the Hunter, was found in years ago. When old Bartushek first came here, he tried to start a mushroom business in some of them, but he didn't make a go of it. The one I go to, nobody else knows about, and though I'd like to show it to you, I don't guess I will. A man needs a hidden place of his own.

When I was at college — my father went to Williams, so of course so did we three boys — I studied history, I wanted to be a teacher. Not like that Leftist fellow, Paul Endicott, though, who used to teach in the Regional High School. No, a real history teacher, and I wanted to teach in an Indian School, like Carlisle or someplace, did you ever hear such a fanciful notion? My father, though, pointed out how impractical that was. By the time I graduated, the Depression — though we weren't as badly hit by that as the Longyears were — was long over and Father had expanded our business. "You must come back to where you're needed, my boy," he told me on Graduation Day, "and carry on the family business *and* the family name."

Of course I saw he was right. But things don't always work out as planned, as the poet said. Neither Lucius nor I had any sons to carry on the business or the name, and young Luke, our younger brother's son — the brother who ran away — is worse than useless. As for Sonny — that's what we used to call our younger brother, but of course he's old now — I once tried to have him traced (though I never told Father) but the detective fellow lost track of him in the Bowery in New York City.

So that's how it goes: no sons to carry on the Hebberd line. And as for the business, I don't really like it. Not even very good at it. It's Lucius has the head for it. He's not only an excellent businessman, but he likes people, even likes serving behind the counter, really *enjoys* it. So I do the ordering and the bill-collecting. Don't enjoy that. Lucius has progressive ideas too. He'll really make something out of this town. "Trouble with you is, Marcus," he often says to me, "is that you like it the way it is." And you know, that's the truth. This is the way I like it, especially after the tourists go and the leaves start to turn.

Now, there's your path: see that little track off to your left? Follow that till you get to the river, there's a bridge of sorts for crossing. Then you'll come to the old quarry. Mind the poison ivy. And good day to you.

INTERLUDE

THE MARBLE QUARRY

The river is a brook here, and the brook rushes along,
rapid over rocks and boulders, then
broadens out into a quiet pool, clear, sun-dappled,
only half-shaded by overhanging ash, ironwood, maple,
flickered with light, a few fallen leaves lazy on it;
clear right to its gravelly bottom, where a speckled trout
only half hides himself under a ledge of limestone.

The bridge is a tree-trunk, halved, cut-side up but not planed:
very rough and too narrow for two feet to be placed
beside each other, and is not over the pool
but over the lively part of the stream
which will surely, in memory, become dangerous rapids,
and the uneven, unrailed bridge will just as surely
be raised over a chasm,
instead of its actual five or six feet above water.

You cross at a wobble with both arms spread out
like a tight-rope walker, and glad no one can see you.
On the other side nothing but thistle and burdock
and plenty of poison ivy. No sign of any quarry
or bit of marble, but a narrow, overgrown path,
five or six cardinal flowers burning red where the path
turns abruptly, and there, in front of you, is a high hill,
almost a mountain, with marble outcrops showing
through dense greenery.

At its foot, a small house of dressed marble,
grey veined grey-violet, well built, square, roofless now.
The door, if it ever had one, is gone; the floor is only
tamped earth, never was anything else.
Pieces of rusted iron under an opening show where the stove was.
The watchman's hut? A shelter in winter for lunch hour?

78

But you don't think about the miserable discomfort that
even this shelter could not have eliminated: you only think,
What a wonderful place to live in,
and know that it's been in dreams you've had, those dreams
of shelter everyone must have from time to time...
How long do you stand there, unaware of time or geography...

A crow caws, far away on Mrs. Dwiggins' mountain-top.
You remember that you came to look for the quarry,
and behind the marble house is a wide opening in the cliff,
man-made, blasted out of rock — bare, jagged rock
rises on each side as you enter this gorge or nave,
and walk on thick grass toward its far end.

There: the part of the quarry that had been mined
deep into the earth.

There is nothing here now but a crag, opposite, rising high,
with one white birch tree growing aslant on its tip,
and silence. No work, no hammers or chisels,
no voices shouting over sledge-blows. No trace.

No bird song, even (for what bird would come here?),
only, between the entrance and the quarried crag opposite,
the pool.

The sides of the pool are dressed marble, giving the effect
of a sumptuous Roman bath — or would give, in more
protected surroundings.
Ledges descend steplike at one of the sides, and into one
of the ledges a clump of wild iris has succeeded in growing.
The pool's water is utterly without movement,
shares — excels — in the silence which is the spirit of this place.
It is deep blue, metallic, a mirror that stares like an eye.
It is no more than twenty feet across, but vast
because its surface tells you it is depthless.

There is no memory of men here, no echoes of voice or tool,
the pool has devoured even their ghosts.

Nothing breaks the silence, no breeze ripples the water,
no cloud crosses the sun.
But you shiver, and walk away as fast as you can,
skirting the marble house where you no longer want to live,
and run toward the river.
And you think, like Lapidus: Who would swim here?

Running across the hewn bridge, back to the railroad tracks at last,
you wonder: how to describe this place?

19. THE STOREKEEPER'S BROTHER

ANCHISIO VARCONI

Emmet McSorley was the only friend I had around here at one time. But before that, I'd always thought a lot of him. When I first got out of school, he was quite the gay bachelor — worked hard all day and danced half the night.

That's hard to imagine now, I suppose. Him being so heavy and slow and swollen in the joints — moves like an elephant, Dee puts it. (Got a memory like one, come to that!) And just that little fuzz of hair on top, like Dee's old kewpie doll. But you can still tell by his eyes, that dark clear blue (they look awfully blue to all us brown-eyed folks) with their piercing look, or that bright twinkle. Except when the blackness comes over him.

Mamma wouldn't let me go work in the quarry. No question, that's why I'm still alive. Nearly all the boys of our kind that I went to school with — the schoolhouse here in the village, and later the High School in Afton, though the most *they* ever got was a year or two there, if that — well, nearly all of them, including my own younger brother, who just wouldn't *go* to school, they all got killed when the quarry filled up. How Mamma did it, Dee and I will never know, but someway she squeezed enough money out of this store and the rooming-house upstairs, to send Dee and me to the Junior College in Albany. It was the talk of the village for years, no question! I studied pharmacology and Dee secretarial work. We both got good jobs after, Dee in the office of the paper mill in Melville, and me in the drugstore in Afton, which I now own and still work in every day but Sundays when I come up here to help Dee.

How does Emmet McSorley come into it? Well, when I got out of Junior College and came back, I found it pretty dull here. I liked my job, but otherwise was pretty much at loose ends. One day I came across Emmet McSorley sitting on a bench in front of the Courthouse in Afton eating his lunch. "Say, Ankie," he said, "why don't you join our club? Handsome young fellow like you would be a good addition." The only club I knew about was that Italian-American Club behind the Meeting House, where all the workers from the quarry and the road-gang sit around watching baseball on TV and getting blind drunk. "What's your club for?" I asked Emmet. "Why, lad, it's for dancing. It's right here in Afton, every Friday. You put on your best bib and tucker, and bring your best girl. Or if you haven't one, come by yourself, for there's plenty of pretty young things there by *them*selves having told their fathers they're going to the sewing bee. And it's not barn dancing, either — waltzes, foxtrots and quicksteps, just like tony folks in Boston. Myself and two of my cronies here in Afton — nobody from Stonecrop, naturally," Emmet said, "we started it last month. We call it the Mayflower Club, on account of nobody in it came over on that large ocean liner."

I remember every word he said, you see, because I'd never had the chance to talk to him before. And of course I joined that Club, and in fact helped him run it. I took Dee with me, as she was surely my best girl in those days, and that's where she met her husband may his soul rest in peace.

Well, Emmet was really a joy to behold at those dances. He was tall and strong but not heavy at all, and a very graceful dancer, his hair was thick and that light red some Irish have. He always had a flower in his buttonhole, and a nice-fitting suit — not like those raggedy things he wears now that come out of the Catalogue, and at that not often enough...

Dee had a terrible crush on him — no question; lots of the girls did, but Dee wanted to marry him. Johnny Ghitalla wanted to marry *her*, but she had eyes only for Emmet. But Emmet was often heard to say that he wasn't the marrying kind, though he never said why. It wasn't any of the usual reasons — oh, I've read the books we sell in the drugstore, especially the psychology ones. No question, in my mind, it was because Emmet could never have found, at least not back here in Afton County, any woman who suited all sides of him. He had that Irish love of gaiety that he'd got from his mother, and maybe his love of people of all sorts from her too. But there was much more to him than that.

He educated himself, nights after work. I've heard say he even wrote a history book. And when he was younger he used to go to New York City and go to plays and musical concerts. Why, nobody from Stonecrop ever goes to New York except the Foleys and that to get in a crowd and see Macy's Christmas parade! Oh, Emmet was a puzzle around here, no question. If he'd been born in different circumstances and in a less hole-in-the-wall place, he might've done anything...

Anyhow, that dancing club went on for ten years before it fell apart. That was for two reasons. The blackness started to come over Emmet, and the war came and I went away. Those spells of blackness came from his father, God rest his soul. According to Emmet, that's as much a part of some Irish as the red hair or the love of dancing.

As for me, I was sent to Pensacola and that's where I met my Southern belle whom I brought back here as my bride.

Didn't I say Emmet was the only friend I had around here at one time? He was the only one who seemed to understand why I'd married that girl, or to try to understand *her*. Dee couldn't abide her and her fluffy ways, she had no friends in Afton, and the winters and the rocky landscape depressed her. She was jealous of Dee, and now that I know more about these things, I can only blame myself for that. Those were the real reasons she ran away. I know you'll have been told all the old gossip already, so I don't mind talking about it, and maybe setting the record straight.

It's true she ran off with that shoe drummer from Boston and also that she took all my savings with her. But the real reason was what I said. I should never have brought her here. And we quarreled a lot. That last time it was about a pair of red shoes she wanted. I said they were too expensive, but to be honest I thought they were too loud and was jealous of other men's eyes on her.

So the blackness came over me too, and Emmet helped me get out of it. He'd take me to New York, or we'd go to auctions with that old cuss Pierre Toupence, and we'd spend nights and nights just talking. Till he got me to understand what had happened. Till he got me to understand that I had to go on living, even without my Southern bride.

And I haven't done so badly. Own my store in Afton, my little house right behind it, was president of Rotary last year, elected to the Board of the Savings Bank recently — the only one, may I say, with a guinea surname. The only thing is, nobody to share all that with, or to leave it to. Except Dee, and she doesn't care about position or have any need of money. Did you know Dee's a wealthy woman? Don't go by the appearance of this store!

Emmet and me, we kind of drifted apart. We have different interests. One of the things he could've got to be is a politician, a Congressman maybe or even a State Senator. But a radical one. Me, I'm conservative. So we have our differences, though I still have a high regard for him. But I'll tell you what I wouldn't tell Dee, she wouldn't understand. Everybody in this world lives separate. No matter what your interests are, or who you have to love and to love you — if you do — the end result is the same. I'll tell you in one word what's the destiny of man: loneliness.

20. THE HERMIT

CALEB HEBBERD

Place suits me. Folks ain't going to make me leave nor the
town bribe me with their handouts. I don't take nothing
from no man, I owe no man. The woods round this shack suit
me. That's where I get my food, see? There's plenty of
berries in them, and eighteen kinds of vegetables that folks
are so ignorant they call 'em weeds, and plenty of good
eating-roots that a man can dig up and store for the winter.
I keep my snares and traps out, get me a nice rabbit, and in
fall I shoot me a deer for winter victuals. There's trout
in the stream, and in summer that's where I give myself and
my clothes a good wash. That goat gives good milk and don't
eat much. Other needs, like store-bought things, can always
be found at the dump. Folks is so wasteful now, they'll
throw out a good frying-pan like this just cause it has a
little hole in it. Easy fixed. Shoes and warm jacket come
from the deer's hide. Don't pay to waste nothing.

Lonesome? Don't have no time for that. Had me a cat once.
Found the creature down by the stream. Strayed, or more
like left there by somebody. Little thing she was, sat on
my knee, evenings. Days, hunted her food. Then like all
female creatures she got wild for a time, took off for a
few nights, and then, in nature's due course, had a litter
of kittens. After that she weren't good company. Nor
wouldn't hunt her food. Stole goat's milk from the pail
and dried meat from the larder. Had to get rid of them kittens. Sacked 'em up and gave 'em to the river. She set up
a howl and a holler. Then scratched me up. "Female in-
grate!" I hollered back. I threw that one out. But she
come back. Howled and scratched at the door. Couldn't get
no peace. So I grabbed her by the tail and cranked her up.
Threw her as far as the eye could see. Never saw her again,
and I'm thankful. I like it better here by myself. Don't
care for visitors, neither.

21. THE THIRD GENERATION

LUKE HEBBERD

I was picking apples — at the Tibbs Orchard on Furnace Road — but it's too nice a day. First I'm going home and have a beer — you want one? I live half a block up Maple Street... I'm going to pick up my guitar here and then hitch into Afton. Maybe there's a movie, or maybe I'll find some of my friends hanging around the Square. There's some benches in front of the Courthouse there. All the old deadbeats sit around all day, summers, to warm their bones and talk about their pals that have died sooner than they have. Now they have something else to talk about: me and my friends. Like our hair and our clothes and all that.

When I was about fifteen or sixteen, I was really square. I washed dishes all one summer at Music Festival Inn so I could buy me a Rolex watch with a wide gold band, and all I could think about was borrowing my uncle's Rover on a Saturday night — when I could get it — putting on some clothes my mother'd bought me, slicking down that short short hair I had, and taking Frank Foley and a couple of chicks that were as square as we were to some stupid tavern. School was awful and anyhow I was no shining light. Frank's mother made him get to be a Scoutmaster, then I didn't even have him around any more. I was so bored I almost dropped dead, and so stupid I didn't even know I was bored. Antonio was always my best friend, but he studied a lot and besides was learning all that woodsman stuff, so as time went on I didn't get to see him much either. Especially after we started going to the Regional High School. Antonio and I had kind of an argument about the transportation. I wanted a car, he said that was foolish — that's the way he talks sometimes. There was a bus, see — you had to get up in the dark and wait for it on a corner, and then sit in it while it stopped at about a hundred other corners. All the kids that were, well, like me, they had cars. Only *my* family wouldn't even think of getting me one.

86

You know about my family? They've got this family tree thing, framed and hanging up in my grandfather's house. Traces our ancestry back to Sir Francis Drake. That's a lot posher than sailing on the Mayflower, now isn't it? My grandfather had three sons — my Uncle Marcus and my Uncle Lucius Junior and my father. My uncles didn't have any sons at all, though, just kept on having a lot of girls. My father had two sons, first Mark, then me. I'm Lucius Hebberd the Third, isn't that a gas? But my father didn't like it here, and about the time I started Fourth Grade he took off. That wasn't the first time, either. He took off once before, before I was born, for a long time. That's why Mark was ten years older than me. Mother kind of liked somebody else, at that time, and she decided to get a divorce. But Grandfather Hebberd wouldn't let her. I guess nowadays she'd be more independent, but it's too late now. In those days everybody went around shaking in their shoes every time the old boy opened his mouth, like he was Jehovah from the Old Testament or something. And Mother'd been raised in just as strict a family as ours, so she never had a chance.

Me? He doesn't make me shake, anyhow I don't wear shoes, do I?

Well all that ancient history stuff I only know from like you say hearsay, because I wasn't even born yet. How *that* happened was, one day my father just wandered back, not a word said, I guess, and then, whammo, Big Reconciliation. I used to wonder how Mother could've been so spineless, but now I figure that it was all a matter of sex. Anyhow, I was the result of the Big R. I don't remember him all that well, because after Mark got killed in Korea, he took off again. Nobody's ever seen or heard from him since. Maybe I've got a bunch of little brothers and sisters someplace. Wouldn't that be something for the Hebberd family tree!

He, my Dad, was a really groovy man, though. Pretty handsome, and he always had a terrific foreign sports car and drove like crazy. Once when we went to Mount Desert for our summer vacation, we had a speedboat and we really churned up that lake. Work? No, he didn't work at all. It was *Mother's* vacation.

She worked in the Store, still does. She's Grandfather's book-keeper.

You'd have thought my Dad's being such a good-for-nothing, like Grandpa would say, would have burned the old man up. But my Dad was always his favorite. (I must say I didn't inherit that, or anything else!) Grandpa was always mean, but when my Dad took off that last time, he got meaner than ever.

Well, like this: you know about the Hebberds? They own every-thing, they've really got it salted away. But they never let go of a penny. I've already told you, haven't I, I'm like the only male grandchild. Well wouldn't you think the old miser'd do something for me? One time I wanted to go to the Music School in Boston — I was still pretty square then: you certainly don't have to go to some stupid Conservatory to learn the guitar — but he wouldn't give. Another time, just lately, I had a really terrific chance: to go to San Francisco and join a group there. "Grandpa," I told him, "this is my chance." All I needed was my plane fare, and I figured he and the uncles would be *glad* to be rid of me, you know? "Sure I'll help you," he said. Well, he gave me five dollars. Honest! "Here you are, sonny," he said, "and all my good wishes."

Couldn't go? Oh no, I went anyhow. I hitched. But I was too late for the job. Anyhow, I didn't like it out there at all. I like these mountains. Out there they call them hills. And I like our winter. Anyhow, those hippies out there are just too far out for anybody like me. And they're hung up on being hippies, you know what I mean? — But as for the Hebberd family... The only time the old boy ever did anything for me was when I got kicked out of that High School. The principal decided I was a bad in-fluence. What? Nothing much. First of all there was the history teacher, Mr. Endicott from New York City — he knew a lot of history that wasn't in our school books. A bunch of us used to hang around his house some. And like every Wednesday we had this thing he called a seminar on the history of Civil Liberties...that was a real gas. Anyhow, he got fired. Then, after I ran my uncle's Rover into a tree, a bunch of us used to borrow a car some place every Saturday night and ride around. It wasn't really stealing, just borrowing. Well, when I got caught there was a big stink. I got put on probation and Grandpa sent me to that stupid boarding-school in Connecticut where Uncle Marcus had gone. A kind of a church school, prayers in the chapel every morning and all that crap, but in some ways it was what Grandpa wanted — "the making of me," only not in the way he like anticipated. There were some fellows there from New York City and they really turned me on.

Then I got kicked out of there — no, not for blowing grass or anything. Besides those god-awful prayers they also had ROTC there. Who needs it? I said. I don't plan to go kill anybody, I said, and so I don't plan to put on a uniform and march around like a horse's ass. Quite a lot of the fellows joined me and we had a sit-down, and I got kicked out.

When I came back here I could hardly stand it. Grandpa and my uncles looked like they didn't have any mouths at all, if you know what I mean, and just *stared* at me like I was some kind of freak or something. Mother, on the other hand, had a great big mouth with all kinds of crying and what'll-I-do-with-you's coming out of it. Frank's family wouldn't let me in their stupid house, and Antonio'd gone away to Junior College. The only friend I had then was my Aunt Abigail. But that didn't work out so great either. Because of why I got kicked out of that boarding-school, she got all excited thinking like I was some kind of crusader or something. Like maybe I was *her* kind of Hebberd. Always going on about the South and that guy King and those students going down there and getting their heads bashed in. I tried and tried to get her to see the difference. What? Well, that it was *me* that they wanted to put on a uniform and like that. But she didn't get it. She's let up on all that stuff now, though — says I've got to like find myself. She encouraged me a lot about my music. And after I'd been back a while I got me a summer job in Afton and saved up and got me my Goya. Pretty soon I found some other fellows around the County that were really into music too, only they were alone and going crazy like me. Well, we got together and got a pretty good group going. Played every weekend around the County and then all over the state and finally in Boston. But then two of the guys got drafted. So it all fell apart. It was just too much of a hassle to get going again.

Aunt Abigail? Yeah, I still go to see her. She's an okay old lady.
But I figure she's just like all the rest of the Hebberds, only in
reverse. You know what I mean?

Me? No, I'm not a C.O. I'm exempt, because of Mark getting
his in Korea. — Why should I feel guilty? If Mark was stupid
enough to stick his neck out... I only feel like sorry. I bet he
was a good guy. He was so much older, I never really knew him.
Grandpa and my uncles are up on cloud nine about him, though.
About how he fought and died for his country, and how if he
hadn't of died he'd be the great upstanding Hebberd and fit to
carry on the business and all that crap. Instead of them getting
stuck with the town hippie. That's what they call me, like in
capital letters. Doesn't it serve them right?

Well, that's enough about *them*. And I've got to be on my way.

22. THE MADISON AVENUE MAN

SIDNEY STONE

Come around to the terrace and join us in a cooling glass of something. We only just got this terrace finished, so the ground's rather torn up around it. There's been so much work to do to restore the *house*, that we haven't even begun to think about the garden. But it's a great boon to have the terrace during these hot, humid afternoons. — God knows what these natives do to keep cool. They never even *sit* on those repulsive porches they've perverted good period houses with. — Now you can see what Patrick Foley, the so-called stone mason hereabouts, did to the lawn back here. You can't trust these local workmen one moment out of your sight. Much less five days out of each week when we're in the city. Earning the bread to restore this place, and may I say to pay them with...

I'll show you the house when it's cooler. Try that chair over there. It doesn't, of course, quite go with the house, but at least it's wood and not metal — friend of my wife designed all these chairs: Shaker adaptations. We're drinking *sangría* this afternoon. (Petronella will be out again fairly soon.) I picked up the recipe in Spain last year. Only we use a decent brandy in it.

Was *that* ever a mistake! Going to Spain, and leaving that impossible McSorley fellow — a carpenter, or *says* he is — to work his will, or rather his ill-will, on this place. Everything he touched had to be undone and done over. Now we use workmen from Afton, but they aren't much better.

You'd think they'd be grateful, these natives, wouldn't you, to have someone with the taste and money come and restore one of their fine old houses? And by *restore* I do *not* mean plastering up a few holes in the walls and putting in a flush toilet. I mean putting the house back into its original state. For instance, look up at the roof. We had the ugly asbestos shingles taken off and

restored to slate. Not *new* slate, either: that would have been
anachronistic. I went down to Connecticut and simply *scoured*
around till I found some genuine old slate tiles in a house-wrecker's
yard. Then take the chimney: we knew from our research in
museums and books on old buildings that a house of this period
simply *must* have had a central chimney. We tore down all the
inside walls but never found anything but crumbled mortar. It's
an absolute *crime* how the former owners treated this place. In
fact, we've had as much work *un*doing their disastrous altera-
tions as in actual restoration. (To say nothing of hauling out
their dirt. They must have lived like pigs. I understand they
were farm-hands or ploughmen or something. Dirtier than their
own cows or horses or whatever. Do you know they plugged
up the holes in the walls with old *news*papers, and buried their
garbage, would you believe it, where this terrace is now?)

I didn't mean to get off the subject, but sometimes my blood
fairly boils. In any case, to continue, we went over to Columbia
County and found old bricks. I think the chimney is really
authentic, don't you? Come inside and I'll show you the fireplace, the part that's in the kitchen. Dutch oven and all. We got
the whole megillah from an old house in Rhinecliff and had it
moved here *bodily*.

No, of course we don't use it — we're not primitives, thank God,
who have to cook their stew in an iron pot hanging over a fire,
nor so poor we can't afford a microwave oven. But all modern
equipment is enclosed behind this wood paneling, do you see?
And the wood! It's *Shaker*! As is the wood of the floors, and
in here, in what was quaintly known as the back parlor, see the
paneling on the walls? A Shaker Meeting House was being torn
down up in New Hampshire and I bought the walls and floorboards. Absolutely authentic. In fact, that's what the whole
place is now.

For of course the house was built by Shakers. You can tell by
its shape.

But do you think these ignorant natives know that? In fact, they
don't even *care*. I remarked, didn't I, that you'd think they'd be

grateful for what we're doing? Believe me, they're not. Far from it. They're even *spiteful*. Some of them go around saying it was never anything but a workman's cottage from the start! Well, what can you expect? They live like animals. They probably *do it* with animals, as one has read in Kinsey.

I'm sorry you can't wait till Petronella comes down. She's getting ready for the concert in Afton, which takes her simply *hours*. Gilding the lily, I tell her — and anyhow, who is there to *see* her hereabouts, even in Afton? Petronella, as you undoubtedly know, is a model, was Miss American Tobacco of 1965 and has never looked back since — though we both had a bit of a *recession* when the tobacco ads were so stupidly stopped — and of course her *appearance* is her *capital*... No, social life is nonexistent here, but we'll change that fairly soon. We like it here in spite of the drawbacks. It's a terrific weekend spot for us, and who needs Bucks County or Westport any more? Anybody can go there. *And* does. But here...well, I consider we've really broken new ground. I've got some friends interested, several men from my agency — one's going to buy the abandoned quarry, he's got Johnson interested in putting up a glass house for him; and another's planning to get that salt-box up there on the mountain as soon as that *peculiar* old woman dies.

Yes, this neck of the woods is a real find.

23. THE CARPENTER

EMMET McSORLEY

A notebook, is it? Now, won't that make me a trifle self-conscious?
Next thing, you'll be going around with a tape-recorder, and
that will truly dry up your sources! — Do you know that, until
recent times at least, the Chinese believed that your taking a
picture of any of them would rob them of their souls? — Och,
well, if it's only a few questions you've noted there, then I
needn't get my dander up, I suppose.

But first let's go in the house, might put a few chunks in the
wood-stove. It's puckering up for rain tonight, which I can feel
in my joints. — Now, what are your questions, lad?

Which lawsuit? The one about the Lapidus house? I drew up
some family trees once, like the ones hanging in the Hebberd
or Longyear front parlours — the way some storekeeper or bar
owner frames his first dollar... I'll have a look for them in a moment.

Obediah's mother died young, and his father soon married again,
one of the Codwise girls (the plain one), but to her he gave no
bairn. But what he *did* give her, having made no will before he
was killed in the quarry, was the house and land come down to
him from the first Lapidus, Zachariah the Blacksmith. She too
soon married again — Obediah's stepmother, that is. After Obediah
the Elder was killed in the quarry, she married a sprout of the
Longyear family. From what's called a "junior branch," which
is a genteel way of saying one that's inherited no property... And
they in turn had a sprout. That was Amenia. (Always a mite
backward, poor thing.) So it was that, on the death of *her* parents, Amenia Longyear came into the Lapidus property. Obediah
was still a schoolboy at the time, but his Uncle Zach, the same
who later struck the boy's name out of the family Bible, a re-
clusive sort who lived up-mountain in the woods, well, Uncle

Zach couldn't bear to see that piece of property pass from one family to another — even though 'twould never have been *his* in any case! — and he started the lawsuit in Obediah's name.

The squabbling that went on about it, you'd have thought it was Windsor Castle, complete with Park and Forest. Ten years of legal wrangling it caused, and a dispute that grew into bitter enmity. Property is surely the curse of the world! No, that's not it: men's unenlightened attitude, which makes them *want* property, that's our curse.

And where did it come from, all this property, in the first place? Stolen from the Indians. Are we cursed because of that, do you think?

Thankful I am that I've no kith nor kin to wrangle over *this* little house. A barely "desirable" property which would surely turn into a mansion in the covetous imagination of cousins or nephews and nieces. It came to me after the death of my parents, and where else was I to live? Truth to tell, I was too lazy, perhaps, to move out of it! So here I've stayed, and that I'm a childless old bachelor is also perhaps a good thing. For who'd want to bring a bairn into this world as it is now? "Cannon fodder," we used to say in the old days of Debs. But now, while we make napalm-fodder of others, we send our own young into despair with our power-madness. Ankie Varconi, who reads and half digests a lot of psychology books and is a bachelor himself now for want of the courage to be otherwise — Ankie calls these ideas of mine "compensation," for he believes my black spells to be brought on by loneliness. But such is not the case: it's a part of the temperament inherited from my paternal forebears (who, may I add, were *not* Kings of Ireland), and that's another fine reason to die childless!

But not, like some others, intestate. That bothered me somewhat, for as we live in a property-owning society, a man must do something with whatever he's got... Bothered me until recently, when a fitting solution occurred to me. This place has one or two advantages: its frontage on the river, just where the deep fish-pool is, and its heat and insulation to keep it snug in the winter.

Besides which, it's built sound and, however messy it may be, kept in good repair. So I'm leaving it to Antonio, Sabato's grandson, for his work with the young boys and girls of the village. For, now, the only hope for this war-raddled world lies in its young.

Now then, why don't you get us a couple of those clean glasses you washed this morning, while I have a look through this cupboard?

Can't seem to find those family trees I told you about. Well, it may be they'll surface sometime or another. I drew them up, you know, for my *History of the Houses of Afton County*. No, the book was never published. It falls between two rickety stools: books of somewhat like sort are put out for snobbish reasons and paid for by the folks that own the houses — vanity publishing, don't you call that in New York? — and then there's the quaint type. Quaint old Yankee codgers and their quaint houses: they all live in "salt-boxes," all built before 1776, except for a few Victorian places called "gingerbread," with all that flossy scroll-work that some now find attractive... (People like to collect ships in bottles too!) You know the expression "as American as apple pie" — so often applied to the sort of thing I'm talking about? Well, there's other things American besides elm-lined Main Streets and Bulfinch churches. Like the old Halloran shack down by the Dump, like those workmen's cabins on Maple Street and back by the limestone quarry. Like the shanties in the South and the huts the migrant farm-workers are packed into... In this very century workers on strike for a living wage were massacred, and children were working in coal mines. Children are still working in the lettuce fields... And right here, as recently as two years ago, the wages and working conditions for the men in the limestone quarry, the resistance of the owners to the union, the violence crushing the workers' efforts to organize — like a rock-crusher on a piece of stone... All part of the "American Way."

At one time I had a crew of men working with me, after the Second War, that was, when there was a good deal of building going on in Afton and Melville. I had long ago joined my Union, and when I told my crew that they, too, must join, else I couldn't work with them, and for their own benefit as well, they refused because they were frightened. And surely they had reason to be! Many's the barn burnt to the ground here in those days, and organizers from the city hustled out of town in the night, or a poor man's chickenhouse emptied by a two-legged fox... Most of those men went on welfare, sat on benches all day, became useless even in their own eyes. It took the Frenchman, in the end, to organize the lime-quarry workers, for he'd been through such experiences in the Resistance in France that he'd lost all fear of anything... For me, there were some hard years, when I was called *That Agitator* and left without work. Until one day old Miss Apthorpe-Jones, down in Afton, told me to come and build a new wing onto her house. Miss A-J was without dispute the arbiter of the social world in this county, with famous ancestors, a large inheritance, and a powerful loud voice. "It's a lot of nonsense, McSorley," she said, "you being put in Coventry for trying to better yourself. The businessmen in this town are simply a lot of upstart shopkeepers, afraid of their shadows and for the pennies in their piggy-banks. You're only following the American Way," she says, "and we'll soon show them the error of *their* ways." So that's how I began to work again.

I well remember the day she got the idea for the Music Festival and, as was *her* way, got it started as soon as she'd thought of it. She and the other rich old biddies in the County had weekly get-togethers called the Thursday Breakfast Club — pancakes and fancy eggs and discussions about Culture and Good Works. One Thursday, while I was shingling the roof on her new wing, she skids to a stop in her old Daimler about one inch from my high ladder. "McSorley," she bellows, "come down off that ladder. I have *news*." Well, I'd been burnt by that before: she could spend half a day talking, and then she'd dock my pay for it.

And *next* day, like as not, 'twould be raining, so I'd lose out twice over, while she'd be roaring about how slow the work was going. So this time I said, "No, ma'm, I shingle, you talk."

"You come down, McSorley," she shouts again. "This time I'll pay — it's worth it."

Well, lad, the night before, in her maidenly bed, she'd got the

idea to bring that fine symphony orchestra from the city up to
these parts for what she said would be its summer home. In the
morning she went to her Breakfast Club and, as she reported it
to me, greeted her chums with, "Girls" — they were all as old
as I am now, and as fat — "Girls, I've got a splendid idea, and
I'll need $80,000 to carry it out." By the time they'd finished
their fattening pancakes, she'd got the whole sum pledged, and
phoned up the orchestra manager down in the city and extended
her command-invitation.

In the spring, the first concert hall was constructed — the Festival's overflowed now, as you know, into the huge shed — and
I was put in charge of the building of it. It's a good, sturdy building still, as I often see, off-season, when I go to the grounds for
a stroll.

That morning, at the end of her tale, she outlined her plans for
the seating-arrangements. "We'll sit inside," says she, "the two
hundred of us County people and our guests, and we'll have
benches outside on the lawn, enough for six hundred or so of
you Others."

Och, well, despite her American Way, you can see that it had
strict limitations, and that Miss Apthorpe-Jones was no lover of
the Great Unwashed.

As for my book, perhaps I went about my subject in the wrong
way. I tried to explain something I thought was important from
the standpoint of what I knew at first-hand. Now, what was that?
Why, houses! I've done carpentry on all of 'em hereabouts. Built
new ones, reshingled old ones. Repaired porches, torn down
porches. Found old pegged floorboards under five coats of paint.
Found Shaker rockers in attics and old glass in cellars. Most of
all, I knew the people that lived in them. From the artists who
lived the other side of Greystone to Miss A-J in Afton. From
old Ghitalla (now in the first Hebberd house) to the Hebberd
by-blow in his shack in the woods behind the Dump. How they
inherited the houses or how acquired them. So you see, I came
to have my own theories about social structure and economic
influences. Leastways in one corner of these United States.

Being no scholar and only self-educated, I couldn't write a book on sociology, now could I?

No, I never got that book published, but I'm not striving for that any more, nor do I feel bitter about it. It served its purpose. What? Why, lad, I learned a lot. Not only negatively, about the flaws in my own writing, but how to think straight, how to use my knowledge to improve my powers of reasoning. That's helped too, with the articles I write for a few of the progressive papers and periodicals. Also learned a whole raft of information about old china and glass and old furniture. Not to mention houses and their periods. And from the Shakers, some of whom I came to know well at Mount Lebanon, I learned to be humble about my own work, and my life too. And some of this fairly useless knowledge comes in handy, after all, now that my old joints and my old age pension have caused me to give up carpentry. I go to auctions with Pierre, and help him with his antique business — if you can call it that! — which gives me something to do and also enables me to meet a lot of interesting people. Pierre and I...you find that an incongruous combination? Whyever so? He and I went to school together and lived the same poor, hard lives, we have much in common. Even though he's an unlettered fellow, he's figured out a few very astute things about the state of the world. Besides which, he distills mighty good cherry brandy.

You might better say the friendship between Abigail Dwiggins and me is unlikely. The daughter of Hebberds and the son of an Irish quarry-worker... But despite the differences, we have more in common than most hereabouts. Even though she's a disappointed woman, and needs me at times to keep her spirits up, she's steady. You see me now, cheerful while the flowers bloom and my tomato plants are fruiting. But in the dark of winter and the deeps of snow, the Gaelic blackness is likely to come over me, just the way it did over my poor father. Then *she* raises *my* spirits. And as I have few to talk over the articles with, she's my listener and critic. While for her, as she doesn't wish to publish her writings, I'm her only reader.

Now *there's* a contrast for you! I struggled and strove with my book, which was never meant to see the light of day, and she just goes out in the woods and writes her sketches and verses, any one of which is accomplished and worthy of putting in print. But they'll die with her... Och, the surprises of man and woman! The surprises we all contain! ...There's Abigail, the dedicated Communist all her grown days, throughout the purges, the pact with Hitler, the Hungarian tragedy, everything. But do you think she writes that Workers-Arise sort of thing of the Thirties? Or prosy shrill pieces, that you see so much of right now, about a Vietnam those writers have never seen? Not she! What she writes is, well, lyrical. Well, maybe it couldn't be pubilshed, too much out of the mainstream. But that's not her reason. She claims it's personal, seems to feel it's too personal, and must be kept that way. No, I can't show her Daybooks — her writings and verses — to anyone. Leastways, I'm not supposed to. Still, how can you understand Abigail otherwise, the side of her nature she never shows to the world?

Well, I'll search through these bookshelves again, see if I can find a notebook or two. Though if I do, it must be private between us, agreed? Then I'll leave one out for you, it may be, some evening before you're ready to depart for the city.

24. THE WEAVER'S WIFE

GRETCHEN JOOST

Max — my husband's — gone to Afton, it's his Wednesday class at the Guild there. He teaches weaving twice a week. Big classes, it's quite a fad now. Amenia Longyear's supposed to sit with me, these times, but I'd rather be alone than have to listen to her. Same old theme song every Wednesday and Saturday — about how Obediah Lapidus is "tricky..." I do believe the woman's got a screw loose, two or three in fact. So I usually send her on an errand — to Kroll's for eggs or someplace that will take a while. Then I'm spared being captive audience for her gossip.

Besides, I *like* Obie. He comes up here fairly often, after work or on a Saturday, and chats with me. Even though I don't go out much any more, I feel I know everybody in Stonecrop just from Obie's stories about them. He's really a kind of backwoods Balzac — watching the whole human comedy from up on his ladders and having a good chuckle about it all.

But you'll have to come back tomorrow to see Max. Stay and talk to me? Sure, why not? And there's some coffee on the stove. No, I can get it. Just push my wheelchair over the doorsill. I can do a lot of things for myself, only Max doesn't like to see me fumbling around, so I take the opportunity, Wednesdays and Saturdays, to keep in practice. I can walk some, you know — I practice walking at night, usually — and I've got a neat gadget for my right hand, kind of like that framework thing the blind use for writing, that I worked out and Paul Endicott, who used to live around here, got made for me in Boston. So now I can write. Yes, I guess I could paint too, but I really don't want to. I did some pretty good things once, but I got painted out a long time ago. Only Max was so ambitious, not just for himself but for me as well: I was a kind of appendage, like his house on Twelfth Street that had to be so perfect, where he built that big studio for me. Once we'd moved out of our loft, I couldn't

101

paint any more. That great, big, absolutely perfect studio, just *bathed* in north light (our loft had been kind of dark) — it overwhelmed me. What I want to do, all those years in that town house, was work in the peace movement. Max had so much money then, that I no longer needed to sell my stuff to help keep us going, the way I did in those good days we had in our loft. And there were enough painters, swarming like flies in the Village, but damn few people, back then in the Fifties, that could afford to work for Women's Strike for Peace full time — or even wanted to. Didn't see what was coming, didn't want to see...

But my God what mixed up people we all are! Max wanted me to paint and get famous, sure, but at the same time he was jealous of my work. Never has admitted it, even to himself. But he was... Every time I'd get a show, he'd take on another job, and get a lot more publicity, and more money, and buy some damn art object or piece of furniture. Mixed up is right! Because when I wanted to quit painting and go to work with that group, he absolutely blew his top. The woman who'd started it was in some trouble with the government — well, naturally — from time to time. Exhibitionism, Max said it was, and that no wife of his was going to get mixed up in that stuff, and that it would get him a bad press and all that crap. Well, the matter solved itself when he decided to come and live up here.

Come on in my room and I'll show you my writing-gadget. No, I don't want you to push my wheelchair. I *like* doing things for myself. You can bring the coffee tray, though. You see, Max hates sickness and disabilities. It's true my hands are knotted up something awful, and hardly things of beauty. But damned if I'm going to hide them... But Max, well, maybe it's because he had polio when he was a kid, and he's kind of ashamed of his limp. His whole life he's had to prove he's just as fit as anybody else, if not more so. Like trying to build this house single-handed! In the end he had to get McSorley in to finish it, but he doesn't like to be reminded of that. When people see the way he looks after me, they exclaim about "devotion" and all that stuff. He bends over backwards taking care of me — *smothers* me with care — because deep down he finds these hands and legs repulsive. I'm still a woman, after all, but he won't have anything to do

with me. We live like we'd taken vows or something, but not
from my choice. Oh, I've had plenty of long wakeful nights to
think it all out.

Now, here's the writing-aid I told you about. Neat, isn't it? I
edit the monthly publication for our peace group, write a lot
of it too, and a couple of my neighbors — Mrs. Dwiggins and
Mrs. Lapidus — stuff the envelopes and mail them out for me and
bank the money I get for dues and so on. Of course, it isn't
much, the mailing *or* the dues, as our membership in this backward county is pretty small. Birchites probably have more members up here than we do. In Stonecrop itself, it's nil. But there are
quite a few young housewives and working girls in Afton that
are getting keen. We've started monthly meetings there. Get
speakers for them sometimes. Abigail Dwiggins takes me down
when Max gets balky about it, even though she thinks anything
short of a revolution is useless. Or so she says.

See, this is how the thing works. I don't say it can produce cop-
perplate writing, but my own handwriting would never have
won any prizes.

Now I'm working out a typewriter that people like me could
use. Man from Underwood in New York comes up to help with
it. I read about a dog out in California — it would be California,
wouldn't it! — that can type on a special machine they made for
it. If a dog can type, I guess a crippled human can!

Brave? What's brave about it? You can't imagine how it is to be
an invalid. Like being made into a monument or something. This
way, I can at least be of some small use in the world.

25. THE ARTIST WHO WAS CIVIC-MINDED

SAMUEL BENNETT

I've stayed up here year 'round for so long I count as a native.
First got this house in 1946. It was a mess. Never was any great
shakes, either architecturally or the way it was built. No proper
foundation, just some dug cellar under the kitchen, and crawl-
spaces under the front, so you could hardly get at the rotten
joists to fix them. The place had been stripped – no doors or
windows or anything. The plumbing fixtures weren't stolen as
there *was* no plumbing. There was an old dug-well down cellar;
Emmet McSorley – he wasn't so huge then – stumbling around
down there in the dark, he fell into it. Wasn't very deep, though.
I worked hard for ten years to get the place in shape. Thought
I came up here to paint, but became my own handyman, even
carpenter and plumber after while. You name it, I did it. But it
was still ramshackle. I considered selling. I'd got caught up just
in fixing it, my work suffered – and I'd learnt first-hand from
all these ingrown Yankees, that it doesn't pay to get obsessed
with property. But then I sold a couple of paintings to Union
Carbide and another to a museum in Iowa or someplace, so I
had enough money to get this studio built onto the house. It's
snug and warm in the winter and air-conditioned in the summer.

First time I came up here in the winter was to vote. The way
this Township is run is a disgrace. I have to pay taxes here, so
I've got a right to say what they go for. By 1950 or so there
were some twenty other people with studios in the neighborhood,
other painters and a few musicians from the Music Festival,
who'd renovated old places just like I had and were paying taxes
just like me. I was always civic-minded, used to belong to ADA
in New York and the Save Washington Square Association. I
rounded up all these others, or those that were in New York,
which was most of them, and chartered a bus and we all came up
here and voted.

It was so pretty, that November, I decided to stay.

But no matter how many of us educated people vote, those illiterate Italians still get elected to mismanage this Township.

Now just step down here to the river. It's *two miles* from the village center to this spot. Yet look at this water. You can see the sewage in it with the naked eye. And see all that scum? That's from detergents. This pollution is absolutely illegal. I've had officials down here from Boston, time and again, and the Township's been ordered to put in sewage disposal. Every house and store in the village that backs on the West Afton just dumps all its shit and dishwater into the river. Barbaric, isn't it? There used to be trout in this river, but they're all dead.

Two years ago the town was ordered by Boston to have a survey made for alternative remedies — where to put the sewage-disposal plant and what kind to get. Well, they even voted down the *survey*. But what else can you expect? They *said* they didn't want to add to their taxes, but it was pure dirty ignorance. Take that dreadful Borgese woman, for instance. When I went to that meeting with all my water samples and reports, she said they didn't need any advice from trouble-making city people! — How dare you call me a city person, I asked her, after all these years? "The years make no difference," she answered in her rough way, "to city-born attitudes." Then you know what she did? She changed her vote from "yes" to "no," and the next day she took every box of detergent she had in that store and threw it in the river, so I could see it floating by and fouling up *my* section of the water here.

Well sure, I'd like to show you my new paintings, but I haven't had time to do any lately. This summer I've got a photographer coming up three, four times a week to take pictures of the disgusting state of this river.

And here he comes now, so you'll have to excuse me. The current's fast today from that rain, but we can still get some good ones.

Excerpt from

TOWN REPORT, 1970
COMMONWEALTH OF MASSACHUSETTS

Town of Stonecrop, Massachusetts

Warrant for Special Town Meeting

AFTON COUNTY, ss.

To any qualified citizen of the Town of Stonecrop, Mass.

GREETINGS:

In the name of the Commonwealth you are hereby required to notify and warn the inhabitants of said Town who are qualified to vote in Town Affairs to meet in the new Village School Auditorium on Monday the 18th day of November, 1970, at 7:30 p.m. for the following purposes:

ARTICLE 1. To see if the Town will vote to make available by transfer, if necessary, the sum of $15,000.00 from Excess and Deficiency Account for the purpose of hiring a Consulting Engineering firm to determine facilities necessary for eliminating dumping sewage into the West Afton River. This project is ordered by the Water Pollution Control Division of the Massachusetts Water Resources Commission, and is part of a State-wide program to stop pollution of all rivers and waterways.

ARTICLE 2. To see if the Town will vote to transfer from Excess and Deficiency Account the sum of $300.00 for Police protection costs for the remainder of the year.

ARTICLE 3. To do and transact any other business.

Hereof fail not and make return of this warrant with your doings thereon at the time and place of said meeting.

Given under our hands this 14th day of November, 1970 A.D. vote of the Town.

ONOFRIO PETRUCCA

PATRICK FOLEY

BENEDETTO STAGLIANO

Selectmen of Stonecrop

A True Copy. Attest: ONOFRIO PETRUCCA

November 14, 1970

I hereby certify that I have posted true and attested copies of this warrant at the Post Office of Stonecrop and on signposts at State Line, Mill Hollow and Cobday's Corners, as directed by the Commonwealth.

ONOFRIO PETRUCCA

Article 1 was defeated by a vote of 48 No and 32 Yes. Articles 2 and 3 were postponed.

SELECTMEN'S REPORT

All tax-payers who have their dwellings or places of business beside the West Afton River voted in favor of Article One. All tax-payers who do not use the West Afton River for dumping their sewage — *viz.*, who do not have dwellings or places of business beside the River — voted, with two exceptions, against Article One. Of the two exceptions, Lucius Hebberd, Jr., abstained, being as how he had his place of business beside the River but his dwelling-place away from the River, and Robert Emmet McSorley of Mill Hollow, who gave a cogent speech in favor of Article One and stated that, although all the tax-payers of the Township would have to share the burden of paying for eliminating pollution from the River, the reason given by the majority, *viz.*, having had own septic tanks installed at own expense, was a narrow view, and should be broadened to include the health and welfare of the community as a whole, and furthermore of all communities lower down on the River, and, in fact, of the country as a whole. Mr. McSorley's speech was interrupted by shouting and several unfriendly epithets, and order not being restored, Officer Silvernail was forced to break up the meeting before Article Two, *viz.*, the matter of Officer Silvernail's salary, could be voted upon.

ANNE BARTUSHEK, *Secretary*

26. THE POLICE DEPARTMENT

CORNIE SILVERNAIL

We used to live in the old house at the Corners, where the Musician lives now. My great-grandfather built it, and my grandfather, the school-master, "modernized" it. I guess that consisted of shoring up the foundation some and building a new privy. My wife had chilblains all winter from the draughts on the kitchen floor, and I hated the place. Now, you take this house. Maybe it doesn't have white pillars up the front and white clapboards that need to get painted all the time, but it's weather-tight. In case you ever want one like it for yourself, I'll tell you that it's called a one-story three-bedder Cape Codder with full basement, and those red shingles on the outside walls are made of asbestos — can't burn up and don't need painting. I give you this information free and for nothing, because I like to see young fellows get wise to new, practical things. Emmet McSorley can go on all he wants about old houses and all that, but I'll tell you one thing: this is the only house in the Hollow that's *level*.

As soon as we'd unloaded the old house onto that summer fellow and I'd saved up enough from my job in the paper mill, I got me this land. It was an acre of the old Codwise farm, up for back taxes. I hewed down all the trees, leveled the ground with a bulldozer, installed a septic tank and got a well drilled, and then got me a carpenter from Afton to build us this house. — Emmet McSorley? He refused to build it. Said he was too old, but the very next week I noticed him repairing the roof on the Shaker Mill. Smart-ass McSorley, thinks he knows it all, doesn't he? — Well, we've got us combination screen and storm windows, washer and dryer, nice blacktop driveway as you see, gameroom in the cellar, fenced backyard for our kid, everything a family could want. There's quite a lot of old Codwise acres still up for sale, and I expect more fellows of my age — I'm thirty-one — at least, as many as still live around here, will come down here and build modern houses like mine. The wife and

I figure maybe we'll even get a tract here, real up-to-date just like they got out in California.

As there's no police station in Stonecrop, I use our third bedroom for my office. I charge the town for that, but they seldom pay it. Half the time they don't even get around to paying *me*. Lucky I have my job in the paper mill. No, it doesn't interfere with my law-enforcement duties, as most trouble comes evenings and weekends, and anyhow I have my deputy, which this year is my wife.

Main trouble comes from those good-for-nothing Italian kids breaking and entering, mostly in the winter, and from those city people, speeding in the summer. Some used to come from those summer people that live around here. Take that musician fellow that bought our house, for instance. One time I caught him driving by here with bare feet. Driving in bare feet is against the law. So I stopped him and gave him a good big fine. Then that music he has up there every Friday night, real late, after the concert's over down at Afton. Four of them scraping out string music. "Tone it down," I went in there and said, "or you'll *all* get a good big fine." No more trouble out of him. But there's still those hippies on their motorcycles, with all that hair and trying to get into the old marble quarry. I've put up posts and signs, as you can see from down by the bridge, and on Sundays I post myself and my police car there. Or if I don't, I can hear them real good from right here in my front yard. I arrest them and call the State troopers on my two-way, and they come and take them away. Only other trouble is making sure Obediah Lapidus has a hunting license, which he usually doesn't.

Now it being Saturday morning, it's time for my target practice. You never know when a good straight aim will be called for in the line of duty.

Some of the neighbors object to the noise, but I tell them they should be glad to have me around to protect them.

27. THE HUNTER

LITTLE SILVESTRO

Just call me Silvestro,
for I have no right to any other name.
I do not know about my parentage, for my mother was surely
    unwed
and disappeared after giving me birth.
All say my father was a son of one of the wealthy families
in Stonecrop village, but I have never believed that.
Perhaps he was some passing stranger from another land.
And perhaps my mother did not die of my birth, as some think,
but lives here to this day.
Who knows?

It was Emmet McSorley found me, not on some doorstep or on
the porch of the church, but here on this mountain-side,
not far from this spot, during one of his rambles; found
me just inside a cave where some poor folks, no doubt,
had once quarried for marble by hand.
He took me to Stonecrop, to the Storekeeper's house,
and so I was named for the woods I was found in.
And so too, then, I was a babe in the lodging-house
of Mrs. Varconi, who gave me what little care she could spare
from her own brood and the hard work of her store and her
    lodgers.
She was a fine, strapping woman with great energy and much wit,
but all her life she'd had to work like a man,
and she was cold at heart.

I was of course, from that household, raised as a Catholic.
Well I remember the cold wooden boards on my knees, each
    morning
at dawn, and the taste of the dry wafer on my tongue;
the harsh voice of the priest in his box, Friday nights,
demanding my sins.

I could never think of suitable answers, so he'd give me
penance for that. One night, in desperation, I confessed:
"A wafer's a wafer, and will always be that, and to me
is nobody's body." So then I was banished, and that suited me well.
But there was a great to-do from Varconis and Foleys.
— By then I was eleven years old and had been apprenticed to
Foley the Mason. I lived in the workshop and took my meals
at Mrs. Varconi's.

When I could bear it no longer, I ran off to this mountain,
and hid in that cave I'd been born in.
There Emmet McSorley sought me and once again found me, and
took me to live in his house for a time, and then sent me
away to a school far from here.
"Shake the dust of this place from your feet, lad," he said,
"as I should have done long ago. When you've had a fine
education, you can make a life for yourself in some center
of culture and civilization."

I did him proud with my studies, and found me a post
in the great Boston Library. I've no doubt Emmet was pleased,
though he never answered my letters.
But one sparkling spring moring this mountain came into my mind
and refused to be banished.
I could see in my eye the leaves budding and swelling,
the bloodroot showing its petals and the fiddleheads
slowly uncurling.
With my few savings I bought this cabin that was once old
Uncle Zach's. I found the gods of the trees and the streams,
and their children the bear and the deer, the grouse and
the chipmunk.
The gods and their children sleep through the winter.
That's when I go into Afton and work in the school,
sweeping the floors and tending the furnace, to keep
all bright and warm for the young ones, and to take care of
my everyday needs.
When spring comes the old gods awaken and I, like their birds,
return to build them their altar of green boughs and flowers.
There are some in the village who would share what I know,
and they may join if they wish on the great day of spring.

When first I came back I was in the darkness of ignorance.
I'd learnt to hunt as a boy — like all the boys hereabouts.
It was never a girl we most wanted, or a good suit or a car,
but a rifle. Young Foley, he's old now of course and has
fathered a young one himself — that's young Frank —
he bought him a Zipper and gave me his old twenty-two.
Many's the unwary rabbit, the woodchuck or bird that was shot
to the earth by the thing while I was apprenticed to Foley
and went out with the others when free.

It was ever the dream of us all to grow up and each
buy us a shotgun and kill us a deer in the autumn.

So, when first I came back here to live, I bought me
a twelve-gauge which you can see there, over the chimney-piece,
as a daily reminder. I waited impatient for the red and
the gold leaves to fall.
When they came, I crept high up the mountain, to the spot
I'd already observed and where I'd built me my blind.
The wind was just right, blowing gently down to my spot,
and I waited a-tremble for the first light of dawn.
And then came the deer, a fine doe, in her full prime and beauty.
She never knew I was there, and daintily trotted
right up to my blind — started munching the leaves on a branch!
Her forehead was square in my sights and my finger
was firm on the trigger.
I looked into her eyes just at the moment she looked into mine.

It was then that all was revealed.
I knew then that the gods were all there around me,
and that she was their most favored creature.

Now I only hunt men. Not to kill, but to keep them away.
I lay snares and bear-pits, and the gods of the mountain
aid with the queer lights they make in the dark before dawn.
Others may live as they wish, so long as they do not disturb
the peace of the gods and the lives of their creatures.

28. THE OLD ACTRESS

OLIVIA DILWORTH

Seen me act? Not a hope, dear boy! You were in your cradle when I last trod the boards. In fact, to be honest, your *father* would have been in his cradle... I'm a great age, do you see, and my day in the theatre would seem rather *historical* to you, I'm afraid. But they were the days of giants... My husband was an actor-manager. There's no such thing any more — young Olivier tried it once, I believe, most unsuccessfully. My husband was in the great tradition: a bit of a tyrant, no doubt, and frightfully temperamental, but what an actor! — and a genius at production: he had *flair*. There aren't real plays and real acting nowadays. Shabby little productions with timid, shabby little people mumbling their words — words better unspoken in any case. Don't know their craft at all.

No, I suppose I've not lost my accent: one doesn't, you know. The folks hereabouts think it's rather queer, but to them anyone who isn't bred in their own county, their own village in fact, seems foreign, so an Englishwoman is no more queer to them than a New Yorker.

Those were marvelous days at Drury Lane. I started out as understudy to Dame Madge, who was my husband's leading lady in those days — and no doubt his mistress as well, as he was a devil with the ladies — and though I never had had to go on, I lived in mortal terror of him. (He, of course, had never noticed *me*: that was long before he became my husband.) But then he began casting about for a new Juliet. Dame Madge had decided to retire while at the height of her glory — such as it was; his complaints about the usual age of the leading ladies playing Juliet (Ellen Terry was the most, well to be kind let us say, *remarkable* for that) may have had something to do with Madge's decision... In any case, he was casting about for a young gel with a certain amount of training, and her own hair — long, blonde hair, do

113

you see. Well, my dear, of course that young gel was *me*. Sounds romantic, doesn't it? I assure you it was little but grim, hard work. I'd meet me friends on Bond Street, perhaps, or at tea at Fuller's, and they'd ask, "What are you playing now?" and I'd say, "We're rehearsing." And then next time, again: "Still rehearsing...?" It became the joke of London. But at last he felt we were ready. And we were a great hit. But all I remember about that opening night is sheer terror! And, at one point, his rage. We were stage centre front with a baby spot trained on us, in the scene where he's saying, "Night's candles are burnt out, and jocund day Stands tiptoe on the mountain tops" and takes me — Juliet, I mean — in his arms. Suddenly I felt a simply frightful pain in my scalp! He was pulling at my braids — that long golden hair that was me *own*, you'll remember! — and all the while looking so tenderly into my eyes in his five-beat pause, he was hissing into my ear: "You're in my light, you bitch!"

Oh, he was a real devil in some ways. But of course he had his other sides too. Perhaps not what middle-class people would call a good husband, but a marvelous lover — and never a dull moment in our forty years of marriage.

For we soon did marry, and played everything: Shakespeare, Sheridan, Shaw, Wilde, Ibsen, Chekhov, some moderns that were coming along then — the new Irish playwrights, Bridie, Maugham... Others, we thought a bit light-weight, didn't touch them though they later became very popular. Even before the second war came along and changed everything, our star had begun to set. Though *he* never saw that: his one blind spot, you might say.

The years pass so quickly! *Tempus fugit*, as some Roman said. One day you're playing Juliet for all you're worth, and the next it's time to play the Nurse. (Perhaps Dame Madge was right to retire at her peak: *she* never had to play the Nurse!) We began to go on tour — that's always a sign of decline, don't you know — longer and longer ones, to more and more distant places, even *Australia*, my dear, where we spent an interminable year. It was late in '38 that we came over here. We weren't liked, you know. They didn't care for our style. Cared more for those Barrymores, perhaps, who did most of their acting *off*-stage... However that may be, our notices in New York were respectful but cool. Not good box-office, that. We had a lovely young Juliet who was much admired — and later became a rich Hollywood player — and I was amiably treated as the Nurse, but *he* came off badly, was thought too old for Romeo, and too mannered. *Autres pays, autres moeurs,* my dear, but the trouble was we were stuck in the "other country," as, whilst we were on tour — a disaster! — after playing New York, the war had come on. We were stranded here; we were, you might say, refugees. That, and the disgraceful way our *Hamlet* was received, broke his spirit. He took to brooding. He began to lose his memory. I was offered a contract in Hollywood, which I took, as we needed the money. — One could get no money out of England by then, do you see. — I spent four years playing sprightly English ladies who were genteelly saving Britain. And *he* simply went to pieces. Simply pined away and died.

My son... You didn't know of my son? I retired for two years in the early Thirties, to have a family. My son of course came over here to join us at the start of the war — a mere schoolboy, he lost, one might say, his background. He became completely American. And, do you know, he had no feeling *whatsoever* for the theatre. It's my belief that he loathed the profession. He became a *physicist!* Fancy that... Rather a famous one, in fact; he wrote a book that's used in classes in colleges. Never could read it, meself. He taught at Williams College, you of course know of it, which is situated in the most utterly cold spot imaginable about forty miles from Afton.

That's all a very roundabout way of telling you how I come to find myself in this spot, isn't it?

My son married a charming French girl whom he met whilst studying abroad, and they had two splendid sons. I'd lived in New York ever since my husband died, I still do, and often came up here to visit my son in the summer. Once, after attending the Music Festival and then motoring about the countryside, I saw this dear little school-house. Quite abandoned it was, but charming — and for sale. The countryside, you know — it was full summer then — quite reminded me of Buckinghamshire, where I was born.

"I shall buy that for my summer retreat!" I said, and I did — then
and there. It seemed ideal, do you see, as being near enough to
my son and his family to see them occasionally, yet not near
enough to become a nuisance. Or to have those two boisterous
grandsons become *overwhelming*. Since the death of my son — he
was only just over thirty, he had cancer. Yes, it was a great
tragedy. I was very fond of him, though I didn't in the least
understand him. My daughter-in-law still lives in Williamstown,
where the boys are now students. She's most kind to me, quite
devoted, and has asked me to live with them. But I prefer to be
on me own.

I see the shadows of the maples have lengthened out: it's time
for a drink. Would gin and tonic suit you?
The three of them call on me here from time to time during
the summer. The boys are interested in the theatre — but it's not
my theatre, our tastes are not the same at all, and they regard me
as a bit of a dodo. Their visits are, in a certain way, a strain. My
daughter-in-law stays with me a week or so each winter in New
York — we do the shops and the galleries and a few plays — as
few as possible, from my point of view! I live very quietly there
in a small hotel. I come up here — just in the heat of the summer,
more from habit than anything else. Yes, the quaint little place
indeed seemed ideal when I bought it: how was I to know then
how lonely it would be?

Yes, I admit it's lonely too in New York. When the boys were
small I used to have them down for their Christmas holidays,
we'd have a high old time: the circus, ice-skating, pains in the
tummy afterwards from those rich cakes at Rumpelmayer's, and
hours and hours in Schwarz's choosing toys... But I don't ask
them now, we're not at ease with each other. It's not their hair
style or those odd ragged clothes: after all, Englishmen have had
long hair more often than short. It was that ghastly Cromwell
that introduced cropped hair — and look at what *he* did. The
clothes must be a protest against something or other, a passing
phase and can be disregarded unless too *smelly*. And the social
protest, as it's now called, in which they're involved I quite ad-
mire. After all, I was a suffragette in me own time, and even spent

a few nights in Holloway for it. Of course, those boys don't even know what a suffragette *was*. They think history dawned with *them*. No, it's none of those things that create a gap — gap, it's a bloody chasm! — between us. It's an attitude toward life and one's profession. In that way I am, as I was born, a Victorian. One must respect one's work, whether it's painting or acting or shoemaking, and the talent one was given... In that way, do you see, the world is now strange to me.

Ah, it's a great misfortune to outlive one's own time.

29. THE YOUNG BARBER

JOHNNY (GIANBATTISTA) GHITALLA

Do you want just a trim, or a regular? The price is a dollar and a half, either way. Makes no difference to me.

My father could tell you the whole history of this town, start to finish, but it doesn't interest him any more. He likes to sit out there on that bench in the sun while he has the chance. All winter he has to stay in, sit beside the stove. In summer he just soaks up a little sun, and watches the tourist-ladies getting in and out of their cars. These new miniskirts have brightened up his life. Doesn't hurt anybody, does it? Little enough after the life he's had. Came over here, steerage, from Sicily when he was nineteen, bringing his wife and baby, my older brother, with him, worked in the marble quarry, lived right here, upstairs, and started this shop down here. He walked to the quarry every morning, walked back every evening, and did the barbering at night. Learned a little English, got his papers, raised us as good Americans, which is now what we all are, thanks be to God and to him.

After some years had gone by, and I had my growth and could help him after my own work, we were able to run this shop full time. But it was hard going. All of us young ones were working by then. My father had seventeen children, twelve of which grew to man (or woman) hood. He saw that all of us boys got some schooling, more than he'd ever had in the Old Country, but in spite of that there weren't any jobs here for us but ditch-digging or quarrying. My oldest brother, the one born on the other side, entered the priesthood, the next went out West to Detroit, two more were killed in the quarry, and another in the War. So that left only me, with a flock of sisters all needing a few dollars for dowries. My oldest married out of the Church and lives in mortal sin, so she needed nothing nor would we have give it. Another sister entered a convent. But that still left us a family of six mouths to feed, and doctors to pay for my mother who was

118

sickly then. To live in that way grew more and more mean and discouraging.

And I too wanted to marry. I'd cast my eye on Delitta Varconi, she lit up a spark in me, and I still believe I lit one in her... But how could I undertake marriage and family, with the family I already had?

Dee tossed her shining brown locks at me, said a girl couldn't live on promises, started going to that Emmet McSorley's dancing club, which was a scandal and blackened her name. She ran after that Irishman something shameful, but in the end it was Borgese she married. a real *vitellone* — a good-for-nothing idler. He had a job at the paper mill. But he hardly ever worked at it. He spent most of his time in our Club. Dee did all the work, worked at the paper mill by day, helped her mother — the old *amazone* — by night. A great change from her dancing days!

She's still the best looking woman in the village, but I'm glad now that things turned out as they did. At first I didn't think so, of course, but I had too much on my shoulders to mope or pine for long. For it looked like we'd have to close up the shop and go to work on the road. The quarry was shut down, the Depression was deep, half the men in the Township out of work. All needed haircuts, but almost none could pay. Then my father has his great idea. Depression-time it was, but it was also Prohibition-time. We'd always made *grappa* in our cellar, under the shop, for ourselves and our Club. "We'll make gallons and gallons," my father said, "and sell it all over the County."

Our troubles were over from then on. I should say that Dee's troubles were over too. She left her job at the mill, took all her mother's savings, mortgaged their building, and bought an old barn over at State Line, and opened a speakeasy. *E vero!* Half that barn was in Massachusetts, and the other half was in the state of Vermont. Dee made it real pretty, with booths and soft lights and a dance floor with music with a victrola. And we supplied her with a lot of her liquor. We all got rich!

Here's how it worked: Dee put the bar on rollers. When the revenue men from Vermont would come raiding she'd wheel it over to Massachusetts, and when the Massachusetts men came she'd wheel it back to Vermont.

She enjoyed it: she's a good businesswoman, and likes a lot of activity. Maybe it's her foreign blood — those Varconis are not Sicilians, you know, but *Piemontese*. Dee's mother was as bossy as she is. And it was rough and no fit place for a woman in that speakeasy. That's why I say I'm glad now that things turned out as they did. I married my third cousin, a quiet girl who wants to stay home and live as a woman should. I can say — *verissimo* — that I have no regrets.

In fact, I have a good life. The shop does all right, and I look after our flag, there on the corner, morning and evening. I have seven children, all boys — oh, they get into mischief, one time and another, but what good American boys don't? My wife gives no trouble, I have the best house in town, and comfort in his old age for my father.

30. THE HOUSEWIFE
VITTORIA STAGLIANO

No, I don't mind talking to you, be glad to talk to somebody. This is a lonely place... We'll sit here on the patio, even if it is clouding over, as it wouldn't do for me to ask a handsome young man into the house in the middle of the afternoon. If old lady Sabato on that side isn't watching me, then that Mrs. Foley on the other side is peeking through her lace curtains.

It's pretty to have a patio, isn't it? Everybody else on this road and up in the village has a porch. They'd call it their status-symbol if they knew the expression. All a porch does is make the front rooms dark *all* the time in winter. But they can sit up high on their porches and watch their neighbors. I had ours torn down, and Antonio Sabato helped me build this patio and that outdoor fireplace, like the one I saw in *House and Garden*, that you can use as a barbecue. Only we never use it. That's the first thing I did here — tearing down the porch and all — that made them say, "She's different." By different they mean bad, you know. Then my clothes. Like these Bermuda shorts and matching shirt. All those other Italian women wear *house*-dresses — the Lord only knows where they get them — or more of the time, maternity dresses. And that's another thing, "Italian." Where I went to school in Birmingham, Michigan, right outside Detroit, we weren't Italians or Irish or Poles, we were American girls, or we thought so. But it's all different here. This place is like a ghetto — you know? — and the Italians keep it that way. And keep their women a hundred years behind the times.

So you can see why I say it's lonely here. And there's hardly anybody left that's my own age. I'll be thirty next year — the Lord only knows how *that* crept up on me! There's only half a dozen couples, and two or three unmarried fellows between the middle-aged ones and the young ones — and those kids will go as soon as they can make it. My husband came out to Detroit,

121

after we got engaged, but he didn't like it and so we came back
here after we got married, and now I'm stuck.

Mr. Ghitalla, that they all call the Old Barber, is my grandfather
— didn't you know that? The summer after I graduated, I came
here to visit him. That old house the Ghitallas got is beautiful.
I'd never seen anything like it before — the house my folks lived
in, and every other house for miles around, was just like that
one Ernie Silvernail built — nor I'd ever seen real country before,
either. I thought it was romantic! And I thought all the dark-
haired Ghitallas and Staglianos were too. At first Vincenzo —
he's now Vince's father, and Vince, you know, is one of this
band of juvenile delinquents we've got here — at first he gave me
a big rush, but I fell in love with his younger brother. Or thought
I did. And I guess he thought *I* was romantic, coming from a big
city and educated and all, especially when that was the time he
wanted to get away from here... But it turned out he didn't want
to get away after all, and didn't really want me either, though he's
never come right out and admitted it. But I know he'd have been
happier with one of those women that have babies every year and
live in their kitchens.

After our baby died and then I said I wouldn't have any more if
I had to bring them up in Stonecrop, he turned against me. He
goes over and gets what he wants every Saturday night in Hudson and I...

Well, I saw you talking to my uncle, Johnny Ghitalla, in the
barber shop... He didn't mention me? I suppose he told you all
about those seven fine boys of his — what a laugh! They're the
main reason I won't have any myself, no matter how much the
priest goes on at me. Uncle Johnny's sons are the leaders of that
gang of vandals. That's all they've got to do around here. Or
that's what they think. Antonio Sabato and Frank Foley aren't
like that. But Uncle Johnny despises them, and as far as he can
see, which isn't beyond his own nose, *his* boys can do no wrong.
Three years ago I was called for jury duty and when they wrote
down Vittoria Stagliano, *housewife*, I felt like my end had come.

After I'd finished high school, my mother wanted me to go to a secretarial school, but I wanted to be a model. I know I'd have been a success at it. I've still got good legs, haven't I? But my father wouldn't let me, and anyhow I came here on that visit and then got married and came here to live. Dee Borgese — she's about the only friend I've got around here, even if she is so much older — she got me a job in a store in Afton. She said I should be more independent, she said that's the great advantage of being born in America, that you could get your independence, "even if you're a woman and live in the crummiest town in the whole country," she said. But I didn't like standing on my feet all day and working in that store. And my husband was dead set against it. He has a pretty good job now in Melville and last year got elected to the Town Board — though that's a laugh, too: he drinks an awful lot, you know, he's drunk most every night these days, and Town Meeting nights are certainly no exception! — well, he didn't want people to think his wife had to work. He said he'd give me my own car, to have all for myself, if I'd quit that job. So I did. Dee was pretty cool to me for a while, but the car gave me more independence than that job did.

But, as I said already, when I saw them write down "Housewife..." Well...

But you never know, do you? For it was that very summer that I...I met somebody. Now my life is all different. I don't want to have to give up my religion, but all the same if you truly love somebody, how can that be a sin, no matter what the Church says? Since I met my...my friend, I'm more cut off than ever in this mean little town. Because no matter how careful we are, of course all these ignorant gossips know all about it... And the winters are more awful than ever — *he's* only here in the summer, you see. But soon I'll make a real scandal for them to chew over! As I said, true love can't be a sin. Pretty soon I'll go away with him.

He's a musician, you see, plays in the famous symphony orchestra that comes here from the city every year — that's the reason he's only here in the summer — and I don't see why I can't fit into that musical crowd just as well as anybody else. I've been watching the musicians' wives for two years now. A lot of them are awful frumps! I've still got my figure, and what my mother used to call my clothes-sense... Oh, I just know I can hold my own at those musical parties they have all the time — they have some down at the Corners, you know, though that's not where *he* lives. He has a place in Afton, and I've watched them going in and out of there plenty of times. Especially now that I'm taking a course in Music Appreciation. It's all on records, and you send in a written test at the end of each part. I've already passed Part Three now! I play them in the winter. It helps to pass that dreary time, and fits me for my new life.

Yes, I've made up my mind: I'll get a divorce and we'll get married, and then I'll have a real life in a real city.

31. THE PEOPLE FROM OUT-STATE

MRS. REDPATH

MISS AMY REDPATH

CAPTAIN AMOS REDPATH

Mrs. Redpath

˙ See him out there digging up the tansy? Some of these country people make tea out of it, or an ornamental edging, but anyone can see it's a *weed*. There's nothing to be done with that slope: it's so full of rocks you couldn't grow any *plants* in it, and at least that weed ties down the dirt. But it keeps him occupied, and keeps him out from under our feèt. Amy and I were *glad* to move away from the sea. Always moiling and toiling, tides rolling in and out, never still for a moment. When Captain left the sea, he came back to Mill Pond, Connecticut, where he'd been born and where I'd long since found us a good period house well away from the Sound and the sea but, fortunately as it turned out, near enough to the Mill Pond so that Captain, when retired, could acquire a hobby. He called it his clam business, but it never seemed to Amy and me more than a hobby, as it didn't bring in much, and in any case my father left me in comfortable circumstances. Captain went to sea very young, started as a cabin boy on a three-masted schooner. Later, first mate on the windjammer of which he was soon made captain. He looked so tall and well set-up in his uniform, he had so many interesting things to tell of his journeys to far-off places, that I was swept away. My people were of quite a different station in life from the Redpaths, having always been engaged in commerce — nothing to do with ships and the sea. But, as I said, I was young and swept off my feet. Little did I anticipate the loneliness of a sea-captain's wife — or what he'd be like when he *did* come home...

Amy was his baby sister. She was still at school when we married — at Miss Spence's in the city, where I'd gone myself long before her — and when she finished, having nowhere better to go, she came to live with me. We've been perfect companions ever since. We made a pleasant, civilized life for ourselves, in spite of Captain and his coarse ways — even after he retired and was underfoot all the time. Amy paints, you know. As I have few talents myself, I've made it my business to see that she's sheltered from mundane matters, and given plenty of time for her art-work As for Captain, I helped him find his landlegs, in a manner of speaking. He was injured in a typhoon which nearly capsized his ship, out there in those South Seas some place. In any case, steam had come in, the days of sailing-ships were over, so he'd have had to retire anyhow. He was unable to adapt to modern ships... So, there in Mill Pond, Connecticut, I helped him buy the old mill over the Pond, which was full of clams and crabs and oyster beds — the Pond, I mean — and he converted the place into a big covered deck off which he sold the clams and oysters he'd garnered at dawn, with two of his poor relations as helpers. But the town grew and grew, till it became like a suburb of the city. Amy and I couldn't abide it any longer. I put my foot down. "Captain," I said, "it's time to move on." I had some distant relatives in Afton, I found this quite attractive house — that was during the Depression, so Amy and I got it for a song — and here we are. I can tell you, Captain didn't come meek as a lamb, but Amy and I had our way in the end. He's settled in pretty well — as you see, he has his gardening hobby now.

As for Amy and me, we've made our niche here. She has plenty of peace and quiet for her painting. The first year or two she was a little unsettled, but that's long gone now. She's doing a pretty landscape this summer, over in Farmer Kroll's pasture. Of course, we have nothing to do with these peculiar local people — why, they're so ignorant they don't even know our *name* after all these years! — certainly not with those dreadful Toupences across the road. (This house used to belong to their parents, though how they came to build such a refined house, it would be hard to say.) That widow-woman over there with her airs and graces, her blue hair and her fur cape, and that rude old farmer-brother of hers... Quite impossible. A cousin of theirs, across the way, built the ugliest shack — goodness knows what use it could have been put to — the first winter we were here, it quite spoiled our view, and I might have had to go to law about it, but the shack fell down and the man passed on before I was forced to take steps.

Captain, of course, took to that farmer person at first, took to visiting over there evenings and, I do believe, drinking, so I had to put my foot down. No, Amy and I have our civilized pursuits not here but in Afton. I started my Browning Society there — I'd had one previously in Mill Pond — and it's still active. And I'm a member of the Afton Garden Club and the Afton County Improvement Society.

Won't you have some more tea? Amy painted these cups, you know. Sweet, aren't they?

Here comes Amy now, just as pretty as one of her own pictures, and you'd never think she'd been out there with her easel in the hot sun. Though I do make her take a parasol.

Now, I'm due at a meeting in Afton, so I'll leave you with Amy: she can pour out your second cup.

* * * * *

Miss Amy Redpath

Do I like it here? I guess so, as much as I've liked any place since I left school. The school, you see, was in the city, and that's where I thought I'd stay, and go to art school, and learn to paint something besides cows and teacups. However, as Sister (she's really my sister-in-*law*, but she likes me to call her Sister) wanted me to come to live with her, and as I was a minor, left in her charge while my brother was at sea... Well, Sister is a very determined person, so that's what happened. Her ideas of painting were a little different than mine. When I left school, I was just crazy about Van Gogh. Laid my paint on with a palette-knife (which Sister, for some reason, called a trowel), and she thought the results were vulgar. Whether *that* or no, the results in truth were no *good*. I could see that for myself. So, in the end, when she'd say, "Why don't you go out in the garden and make a nice watercolor of some flowers," I'd oblige. I didn't mind all that

much; it got me out of the house and helped pass the time while
Amos was away on his voyages.

Oh, you can't imagine what a fine figure of a man Amos was in
those days! When he'd come back it would be like a month of
Christmasses! His grey eyes that had looked far over empty
oceans, and then at strange and beautiful tropical lands, would
be bright and laughing as he hugged me and whirled me round
in the air, and then pulled out of his sea-bag some marvelous
present he'd brought me. You see that tea-chest? He brought
that — I swear it still smells of the Orient, like this spice jar from
Java.

The most interesting trip he ever took was to Easter Island.
There's a lot of books about it now — I get them out of the Afton
Library — with speculation about the origins of those huge statues.
But when Amos sailed there long ago, no one really knew any-
thing about them. He made sketches of those big statues and
brought them back to me.

And one time he took me out in his great windjammer: we sailed
from Mystic, Connecticut, to Boston and back, we even had a
slight squall off the Georgia Shoals — oh, I love the sea, especially
when the waves pile up in a storm! That trip was the most exciting
experience of my whole life. Do you know that Amos was only
twenty-two years old when he first was made Captain? I went
back to Mystic later on, where there's a docked windjammer
and a museum, and looked in the records. There were quite a
few young captains in the big sailing-ship days — almost before
I was even born! But there it was, right in a big ledger sort of
book: Captain Amos Redpath, youngest sea captain from Connecticut!

I'll tell you what else he brought me. From Easter Island. And
there was quite a controversy, about that present, among scientific
people. He found two *small* statues of gods on that Island. He
bought them in exchange for his second-best spyglass, and brought
them to me. I showed them to a man in the Metropolitan Museum
in New York, and he said they couldn't be genuine because there
were no small statues, ever, on that island. I told him straight

out: "If my brother, Captain Amos Redpath," I said, "Master of the good ship *Sea Lion*, says that's where they came from, then that's where they came from." (Of course, they know better *now...*)

But at that time not a month had gone by when an archaeologist came to Mill Pond, bringing with him a photographer from the National Geographic Magazine, and wanted to examine the statues. But they'd been put away by then. You see, they were gods, but they were also men, male figures, I mean, and entirely undressed. They were the most beautiful workmanship, carved out of stone, and they had obsidian eyes. But Sister, poor woman, thought they were indecent. So she shut them up in a trunk in the attic and locked it. We still have the trunk, up in this attic, right here where we live now. I do believe I'd show them to you. But I haven't the key.

Two gods from Easter Island, that my brother Amos brought to me!

* * * * *

Captain Amos Redpath

Back-breaking work this is, for a man not used to stooping, but I aim to terrace this slope and grow grapes. They grow good wine-grapes over in New York State where it's just as cold as it is here. Besides which, there's some chalk in this soil, which is propitious. I've got all my fancy lettuce sold, and my snapbeans and young carrots. The wife's taken all the prizes for roses and bulb-flowers down at her twittery garden club, and I'm waiting for my tomatoes to ripen. So now's the time to grub out this tansy and terrace me my slope.

Hot out now, though. Come on back to the tool-shed and we'll have a snifter. That's where I keep it so's *she* can't find it.

I can tell you one thing: never thought to end my days two hundred and fifty miles from the sea I was bred on, and find myself hemmed in by a parcel of goddam mountains. "Trains," they call 'em here — something to do with rocks that were shoved around by the Ice Age. They can call 'em trains all they want, but they don't go anywhere. Nowhere *I* want to go.

Where? Back to the sea. Or some island rising out of the sea. Never thought to end my days ashore with a bunch of women, either. *She's* lived her whole life in a parcel o' teacups, and she made my sister Amy, who was a good-looking wench once with some spunk, into her own shadow. Why, Amy even *paints* those goddam teacups.

Wasn't so bad in my Clam House at Mill Pond. Wasn't a ship, but was like the deck of one. After *she* made such a fuss about my working on a steamship, demoted to second officer because I didn't know the ropes, seeing there weren't any, and also another goddam fuss about that bitty wound in my leg, which came from a Chinaman's knife in a waterfront saloon, whatever *she* may believe, I figured to get me a shore job. I didn't like those steamships anyhow — dirty, heavy tubs driven by coal instead of good, clean canvas. Didn't mind being second mate, except for the way *she* went on about it, but I couldn't abide those tubs they now call ships. I was only thirty at that time. Hell, that's a parcel o' years ago, ain't it? So I got the job of Harbor Master at New London. But *she* wouldn't haul anchor. And I got it in my mind that I wasn't doing right by Amy. She's nigh eighteen years younger than me — my Pap was surely a lusty old fellow! — and I was left in the position of being her guardian. I had not rightly guarded her at all. There she was, Amy, living with *her*, and fast becoming an old maid. Just like *her*. Hell, maybe she preens and puffs and likes to be called *Mrs.* Redpath, but she's more of an old maid than any "Miss." I didn't see how I'd ever get Amy out of there and married off if I didn't set my own house in order. So I gave up my Harbor Master job after a few years and went back to Mill Pond. I had plenty saved up. Young sailing-ship captains got big pay, but the real money came from trading. All of us captains'd take a few kegs of rum out to the southern seas with us and trade them for native things. That reminds me: time for another snifter. Nothing like a good tot of dark sailors' rum, is there? Piece of tapa cloth I got out there — and that one was *free*, if you catch my meaning — hangs in a museum in New York City. Got a bundle for that.

I took my gold and bought the old mill house there in Connecticut and fixed it over. Dug clams and netted crabs and raked oysters every morning and watched the dawn come. Sold the seafood out of baskets on my deck. Folks came from all over to Cap'n Amos's Clam House. Evenings I'd swab the deck, clean out my baskets and my punt, and then just sit there, while eating the supper Amy'd bring me, and watch the sun sink behind the Pond. It wasn't the sea, but had its own beauty. Willows grew there, and you could watch the moon rise through 'em. The quawks would come — some call 'em night herons — and fish off the edge of my floats.

When I came back from New London, I brought my young first mate with me. Assistant Harbor Master was his fancy title. Thought maybe he'd take to Amy, and he did. He set about courting her. But nothing came of it. Amy only wanted to trail around on my heels. Maybe it was too late by then, or maybe she just didn't have it in her.

Strange thing is, though, when we first came up here to these goddam mountains, she fell in love with Louis, Pierre Toupence's son. She must have been eight, ten years older than him, and he was no great catch either, nor did they have what *she* would call a thing in common. They had *one* thing, though, as old as Adam and Eve. It all took place over there in Pierre's barn. I was downright glad Amy could become a woman. Lucky, though, she didn't get a bun in her oven, for then *she* would never have stopped squawking. Amy and me would've both got thrown out. Not that I would've minded, but what about poor Amy? As it was, *she* never knew a thing. And nothing come of it either, Louis never took it serious. Pretty soon he married some local girl, big ham-hocked mountain girl, and they went out West someplace. It created a coolness between Pierre and me, however — though I never figgered out why. Pierre's an awful nice fella, taught me a lot about gardening and the earth, and I regret the loss of his company. I always wondered if *she* didn't have something to do with it, maybe went over there and warned them off like they were poachers or something!

How I happen to be *here* is like this: Mill Pond sprouted and

grew, full of city people that wanted to live there at night and
work in the city by day. Ever hear of such a goddam crazy idea?
The result was, a piece of the new four-lane highway was put
right outside my Clam House. The noise and dirt was something
fierce. Interfered with my peace of mind. At the same time all
those city people started clamming and crabbing in the Mill Pond.
And some poachers too used to come nights, out of season when
the oysters were breeding, and even though I'd keep watch all
night and took pop-shots at quite a few of them, the end result
was that, between the lot of 'em, they cleaned out the beds. Now
there isn't any more seafood in that pond. So I gave up and sold
the place to a house builder. When *she* determined to come up
here, I thought why the hell not? There's only one place I want
to be, and that's on an island I know in the South Seas, and I
certainly ain't going to take *her* there, even if she'd go.

So I'm biding my time. What's that? My age? I'll be seventy-six
this winter. Gives me plenty of time. Redpath men were always
lusty and long-living. My Pap lived to be ninety-six. No, *she*
comes from a short-lived family, and what's more has a bad heart,
no doubt from these goddam long winters. So I may be taking off,
any day now, on my last sea voyage.

AFTON COUNTY IMPROVEMENT SOCIETY

in re: Agenda for the September Meeting

Once again, it seems, we must devote most of our next meeting to that thorn in the side of Afton County, namely, Stonecrop Township. First of all, we adjourned our July meeting before the wording of the commemorative plaque to be erected on the site of the old Cobday mansion (after its ruins have been pulled down, that is) had been agreed upon.

It was suggested at the close of the last meeting that our next, after our August break, should be devoted to deciding upon one of the various plans submitted for turning the house of Miss Arabella Apthorpe-Jones (the undersigned's great-aunt), into a museum, as prescribed by her Will and by the Trust Fund set up for the purpose before her unfortunate demise. However, several urgent matters concerning Stonecrop have arisen in the interim.

It has come to Your Secretary's attention that the purchaser of the former Codwise place in Mill Hollow (a house of no architectural distinction, although the property itself is well situated) is an Undesirable. It is rumored that he changed his name to Stone from *Stein*. We all know what that means. Our efforts to keep the Catskill element out of our fair County have been successful as far as the Township of Afton is concerned, but all efforts to gain co-operation from the Selectmen of Stonecrop have been unavailing. It must, of course, be borne in mind what *their* backgrounds are, they themselves being immigrants and foreigners. It is they who, having taken over the old Codwise place for unpaid taxes, sold it to this newcomer without bothering to scrutinize his antecedents or, for that matter, without consulting this Society. When questioned about this dubious sale, one might add parenthetically, a Stonecrop Selectman, one Foley by name, answered brusquely: "The sale has brought income and work to the village." Furthermore, they have for some years now allowed a widow woman, Mrs. Prudence Cobday, *née* Codwise, to live, rent-free may one

133

add, in a most unsightly old tenant-house adjacent to the aforementioned property. (Another eyesore which ought to be eliminated!) The purchase of the Codwise property is a *fait accompli* which, our distinguished legal Counselor informs one, will have to remain so. However, it has also come to Your Secretary's attention that there is an historic building on the mountain above Mill Hollow, namely, the Hebberd place which was erected by the younger brother of one of the first twelve settlers of Stonecrop in 1772. The house is a so-called "salt-box," unique in the area and quite unspoiled. It is presently occupied by one Mrs. Abigail Dwiggins (*née* Hebberd), a childless widow who has already passed her sixty-fifth year and is said to be in failing health. Rather than have recent history repeat itself, and be confronted with another disastrous *fait accompli*, Your Secretary urges that this Society take action *now*. One suggests that we investigate the status of Mrs. Dwiggin's house, and discuss ways and means of the acquisition of the property by this Society. From now on our motto must be: *Carpe diem!*

Yours respectfully,
R. *Apthorpe-Jones, III, Sec'y*

32. THE FBI MAN

OFFICER FLANAGAN OUT OF BOSTON

Federal Bureau of Investigation, and I'd like to talk to you. Identification? Sure. Most don't ask for it, but here it is: that's me, Officer Flanagan out of Boston.

Maybe *you* could help me out. Can we sit down? On the porch? Well okay, but it's kind of damp. Yes, I *know* it's not your house, it's R.E. McSorley's house, but you've been staying here for weeks, haven't you?

I observed that you've been nosing around here all summer, and that people even talk to *you*. That's why I think you could help me. Believe me, I feel funny, coming around like this — it's not the kind of thing we do at all, but, well, these circumstances are unusual, to say the least.

I'm trying to trace that Commie, Paul Endicott, who used to teach in the Regional School and lived up the road, but the trail ends right here in Stonecrop. Don't know him? — of course you don't, he left here nearly two years ago, and now he's just plain disappeared.

The reason he has to be traced is that this place is a hotbed of draft dodgers and disaffected kids, and we haven't a doubt in the world but that it's all due to that Commie Paul Endicott. Vandals? I don't know anything about them, we're not interested in that stuff. It's the draft dodgers, that ignorant old Eyetalian woodcutter's grandson and his pals. They all went to classes taught by that Commie Paul Endicott, he's a known fellow-traveler, and the rot that set in here must've started with him. Why come to you? Well, it's like this. I go to somebody's door and knock and ask, "Do you know the present whereabouts of the Communist Paul Endicott?" Here's what happens: some slam the door in my face, some say, "We don't want to buy anything" and *then* slam the door in my face. Some say, "We don't like Commies but we don't know anything about any Paul Endicott." Some pretend they can't even speak English.

Now a *few* have said a *few* words, and here's the answers, as listed in my notebook:

1. That doddering old fellow, your *host*, R. E. McSorley, "Seems like I heard he went to Mexico."

2. That old woman up on the mountainside, used to be a Commie herself, but harmless now, I'd say, at her age: "How's that? Governor Peabody? I don't know him. *Not* Governor Peabody? Well, I don't know *any* Governors. What? Well, I don't know what you're talking about when you mumble like that. Better come back some day when my hearing-aid's fixed." (How's *that* for a put-on?)

3. That crippled woman in the wheelchair: "I heard he went to California." Her husband, that weaving fellow that has a Jewish name: "I hear he went to Canada."

4. That curmudgeon, Toupence, with that junkyard barn up the road: "You'll have to ask Captain Amos, cross-road. Only you don't want to believe anything *he* says."

5. Captain (but a captain of *what?*) Redpath: "Must've been before my time." (He's lived here twenty years at least.) "Better ask Pierre Toupence. Only he's an awful liar."

6. The Postmaster (and his own son's one of that bad lot): "Got some mail for Endicott stacked up here, no place to send it to. You can look at the outside of the envelopes if you want." (It was all circulars and that kind of stuff.)

7. The Storekeeper: "Never had any Commies around here, wouldn't let 'em into the town if they tried to come. And I'll tell you something, Officer Whatever Your Name Is," she says, "nobody around here's going to tell *you* a damn thing, even if they know anything, which they don't. Around here we don't talk about our neighbors to outsiders."

8 & 9. An old guy named Ambrose Longyear set his dogs on me, and that housepainter kept me standing out in the rain while he thought over my question, then said, "Nope, don't know nothin'."

Now I ask you, how can I go back to Boston with a report like that? It's as much as my job's worth. What do you mean, "What's it worth, anyhow?" It's my job, the way I make my living. I got a wife and two kids to support.

Want to see their pictures? Cute youngsters, aren't they? Well, it's too bad you can't help me. When I heard you were nosing around, I had you checked out and you got a clean bill. So if you *had* learned anything, it would have credibility. Well, too bad.

These people around here really are something *else*.

33. THE MUSICIAN

ANTON JENSEN

We've got a bassoonist — a *lady* bassoonist, I tell you! — coming along later, maybe about midnight, so we shall be playing the Schubert Octet. We have extra instruments tonight: strings never hard to get, clarinet, oboe, the same, horn we got any time, as we're often playing the Brahms, other things, but bassoon always difficult. So, *ja*, at last the Octet. That's to say, if my colleagues in there do not get themselves first too involved with my keg of beer. We have always some eats and drinks after playing, no matter what the hour, but tonight while they wait for the lady, they broached already the keg. So now instead of playing that Mozart Divertimento, as intended, they stand around guzzling and talking about their instruments.

Maybe you think musicians talk about music? Not so. Come in and complete your education if you wish! In any case, let us not stand about out here in the dampness of night. Perhaps, too, you wish to wait and hear the Octet? The lady has good lip *and* is most pretty. In fact, too much so, Clem Palatino — he that I share stand with in the second violin section — Clem is such a, how do you say it, an old goat, been having grand affair each summer with local lady up the road — married lady with Town Selectman husband! — while his wife, she's tucked away in Boston tending babies, so now he casts his eye on the pretty bassoonist... I see much fireworks ahead, but am concerned only to keep my group together. Without it, we few men would be dying of boredom with what we must play all summer here. If is not Tchaikowsky, is Tchaikowsky. Everything the Old Man conducts sounding the same. Only sometimes some surprises. Such as tonight. Wanting to get home to his supper, he takes us through the *Prague* in twelve minutes flat. Sounding like von Suppé. Earlier, he's playing his own adaptation of a Bach prelude scored for full orchestra *and* organ. Sounding like The Maiden's Prayer.

138

And the orchestra, finest-trained body of men in the country, maybe the world: eighty people turned into one instrument...and what does that instrument play? Of course in the winter is not so bad. But still... You can see why I had to start this chamber group. If we were not playing *music* once a week, we'd drop dead or turn into bunch of insurance salesmen.

People can come listen if they want, but that's not the purpose: we're playing for our own sakes, for music's sake.

Outsiders have much wrong ideas about big symphony orchestras, thinking they're dedicated to music. Maybe at one time. But now they're big business. In Hollywood they say: "It's not an art, it's an industry." Same thing here. But more honest there. Our Board of Directors are pretending they make Culture. But just let the orchestra get too far in the red, then, whooo, sparks are flying and management chasing their tails like dogs with fund-raising and getting more recording contracts.

As for us, the "instrument," all we are thinking about these days is our salaries and royalties, and the stocks and bonds and tract-houses we can buy with them.

Yes, some exceptions. Some of us older ones, we remember those days when we only played twelve, then at most twenty weeks a year, and having to take what we could get the rest of the time. We were not so comfortable then, but we were more alive — and we *played*.

Oh, I know well what I am talking about from life-experience. Long life, fifty years old now, in fact a few years more, and hard life, you can tell from my hair. Very white now, no? but still plentiful, glad to say, for I am a little bit vain. And you can tell from my accent — though I like to think I did lose *that* — how I was born in Europe. In Germany, that was, though I am purely Danish. My father's business took him, and so his family, even me, the unborn one, to Berlin, right after the First War — and that must seem, to a *jüngling* like yourself, like another era, another world. And so, of course, it was. I went to the Hochschule in

Berlin. Busch was my teacher. At twelve I was playing solo with provincial symphonies, soon in the capital. But those were bad times, rumblings of worse: inflation-times, Brown Shirt-times... Sixteen, my father took us back to Denmark: soon I was playing concertos with all the great European orchestras, giving recitals, too. Was playing in London when the Second War broke out. Interned, because born in Berlin, in England. *Good* fortune. Anton is no warrior, Viking ancestors or no. Man should live by the bow — or pen or paint-brush, as you will — not the sword. So, bad circumstances were good to me... I was lonely there in the camp, lonely for music, and had plenty time to think. Lonely for what music? I could ask myself. Being soloist was *career*, playing chamber music was *music*. And applause of crowds, whether in football arena or concert hall — oh, very habit-forming. After the war, orchestras were poor, so was Denmark, the quartet I started could barely make traveling expenses. And I had a wife by then, and two children. The old German who founded this orchestra sent for me. I came, came to North America. "You want take over first desk, second violins?" was what he asked. "Got a good Frenchman, trained how I want now, for Concertmaster. But plenty want this chair. You say yes or no now." I knew what my wife would say, and one baby we had, our girl, needed operations on her eyes. So: I said yes. Twenty-two years ago, that was. My God, hard to believe.

At first it was a good life. We had a walk-up in the city near a park, and the season — thirty weeks a year by then, the longest in the country — paid us enough to get by. The little one's operations — I took pupils. Some were good, couldn't pay, others paid plenty for hurting my ears. And I started my quartet again, during our off-season. Hard work, lots of travel, good music.

But now, no chance for that; work in the orchestra all year, make lots of money, play at night after the concert to pretend we're still musicians. When I retire, I'll start my quartet again. Old as I am, my vision hasn't fallen off any more than my hair, and my fingers are strong and steady as ever... Retire! What has that to do with music? But that's what these fat puffers and strummers wanted, with their pension funds and benefits and royalties. I'll only "retire" from the orchestra into my string quartet! I can leave any time — don't need big salary, pension fund, fifty-one weeks a year. Can keep this house — no mortgage, upkeep very cheap, go on tour, live here, anything... My son is college professor (he's no Viking!), nice safe job; my daughter — in a minute you'll meet her, she's here tonight — she's grown up, married, has now perfect eyesight. So what do I wait for? Three more people like me! — with instruments, ready to travel... Retire, stupidity! Remember Maas, cellist in the old Pro Musica? He died right on the platform, someplace out in California, in the middle of a Mozart. That's the way to live, and to die.

You wanted to talk about Stonecrop? What can *I* tell you? I bought this house twenty years ago, when my wife was still alive and our children were growing up. Lived here every summer since. But the "locals," they still pretend they don't know my name — call me the Musician to this day. I understand *them*, though, they are not all that different from Danish farmers: narrow, can't say much, plenty suspicious, but see some things very clear. And what you can't say about many, these times, not torn out of their own earth. One day I'm talking to an old fellow down the road, Pierre Toupence, his name is. "City folks soft," he said. Probably he was meaning to be rude, but I had to agree with him.

You see that young chap in there, the youngest, with the blond hair? He's my son-in-law. Plays cello in Buffalo Symhpony Orchestra. His first job, been there one year. Just arrived here to visit, sniff for job in our orchestra... That saucy-looking dark girl over there, she's my daughter Alice. Takes after my wife, *dark* Dane. Well, that boy, you know what he has done? Bought a Stradivarius! When Alice got here today she was not so saucy. Crying on my shoulder. "It'll take us twenty years to pay it off," she said. She's a good violinist herself, but never had a chance to stretch her wings, been working in an office to put *him* through Juilliard. "Twenty years," she says, "so there goes my chance for quartet work. That cello," she says, "that's my music and my baby and my new living room sofa." Now I ask you, what does a young chap like that need a Strad for? When I was like him, just starting out, I had an old cigar box with four strings on it! If you see old Toupence, you can tell him it's not just "city folks" are soft: so are musicians.

Well, here comes our bassoonist. Now we can find out what living is all about.

34. THE CHURCH-GOER

ETTA TIBBS

People in the city always on the run, running and grabbing after things that are of no account anyhow, as those things are of this world. City man came and took over my Pa's orchard, about thirty years ago it was that we lost it, but that man didn't understand our ways here, nor the ways of apples neither. Now Farmer Kroll's brother owns it. No, I have naught to do with it. I always had a busy life till the Fire.

You've seen the Meeting House down-street. I was never part of that congregation. My great-great-grandparents and some others broke away from there long ago, went down to the Hollow and then up-mountain on the old back trail to State Line, and over t'other side of the mountain found theirselves a piece of clear, flat land with a view of Greystone Mountain, and a valley between filled with maples and firs.

No other people about, nor a dwelling in sight. Simply God's beautiful world all around, and the freedom to worship Him in their own way. There were no rules and regulations about who could come there or who couldn't, or where you had to sit when you got there. No preaching and punishments: man being born sinful in any case, what's the use of all that? Better to praise God in a beautiful place, and try to behave the better for that.

And it was a beautiful place, which they built with their own hands. It was plain and pure, with a delicate spire pointing to Heaven, and many large windows of clear glass to look through at the glory of trees and mountains, of bright leaves or white snow. At first there were few in the congregation, but as folks heard of our ways, more began to come. After a good many years, the Main Road to Albany was put through the village, and a spur branched off, other side of Konkapot Mountain, to Afton, and went right past our Church. That was in my mother's time. Then many folks, even all the way from Afton or Melville, began to come, and then, in my own time, the building itself had many a picture taken of it. But we maintained our old ways: that Church was built for worship, not as worldly architecture!

As for me, as a young girl I ran wild and barefoot in the apple orchard, thought nothing of worship, and was wholly caught up with the things of this world. I even became engaged to marry a young apple-picker, a dark handsome boy as wild and worldly as I was myself. But when the orchard closed down, as I mentioned, he went to work on the railroad, and his mortal body was crushed by a truck gone loose on the tracks.

Then did I see the great blinding light, and soon what my life ought to be was revealed. Our Church had fallen from grace: the roof was in sad disrepair, and the steps had caved in. The congregation had fallen from large back to small as more and more folks left godly ways. There were more people took pictures of it than went inside it.

So it was revealed to me that I should set about restoring our Church. Would it surprise you to know how many folks rallied round? We had suppers and picnics, bazaars and appeals, and at last, two years ago, we'd raised enough funds in the name of the Lord to raise us up a new roof! We had a supper of great rejoicing.

Then came the storm. Up in these mountains, in the heat of the summer, we're afflicted with storms of fierce thunder and lightning.

That very night the lightning struck straight down on our Church, and it burned to the ground.

I ponder and pray, and I pray and I ponder, but my question's never been answered. Why did the Lord strike down our Church? Why did He strike down the work I'd done in His name? Why did He strike down His own tabernacle?

Others have built there a stone platform, and an altar of marble, and some Sundays in summer they hold services there, for no doubt 'tis still a beautiful spot.

But I never go. I wait for my answer, but it's never been given. If you want to, you can keep the picture I showed you, for I don't need it myself.

35. THE STOREKEEPER

DELITTA VARCONI BORGESE &
THE TALE OF THE MURDERED TRAVELER

You won't find anything around here to write a story about. No famous people in Stonecrop. There's that artist that never paints anything — too busy sticking his nose in other people's business — and the weaver that never weaves anything, and that musician that scrapes a few notes on his fiddle every summer... Nothing here for you. There were some famous people in the County once, but none of them ever came near this god-forsaken village. There was that one that wrote the poem we had to learn in school, "Thanatopsis" it was called. Ankie and me and the rest of us couldn't read much English at that time, and had no idea what it was supposed to mean, even the title; it was years before I discovered *that* was Greek. There's a lot of houses in Afton County named after that old guy — he must have slept around like George Washington! — but not a one in Stonecrop. It's like Ankie says, the town looks like it got bombed before any bombs ever fell. Nothing ever happens here.

There is one thing, though, might make you a story. That old guy wrote one other poem I read, and the reason I did is that some people with tongues bigger than their brains said it was about an event that happened right upstairs here where Ma had her lodging-house.

That poem tells about a stranger come to an Inn, one dark and stormy — naturally! — winter night, and about his flashing his wad and being eyed by two other strangers, the bad guys of the story. Stranger eats his supper and takes off again into the storm (he must've been nuts) and pretty soon the bad guys follow him. Said stranger never heard from again. — But if he was just passing through, and nobody knew his name anyhow, why or how would he be heard from again? — However that may be, in the spring when the snow melts, somebody finds a skeleton in a ditch (the body of some dog if you ask me). Anyhow, that's the story, and it was told in the days of the American Revolution, and then this old guy wrote it up in a poem. Now I ask you, how could it have happened in Ma's lodging-house? She lived to a ripe age, but she wasn't *that* old. In fact, that poet fellow was probably dead before Ma ever came here from the old country. Pretty stupid story, if you ask me, and those tongue-waggers are even more stupid, but what can you expect of a bunch of Sicilian peasants?

Emmet McSorley — and isn't *he* old and fat and stiff-jointed now — he told Ankie that the story is arch...arky-something (I can't remember the word, though Ankie knows it), and that there's one like it in most languages and that some Russian fellow wrote it better. Which wouldn't be hard, would it?

Anyhow, while people are going on about that old tale that probably never happened, there was a *real* mystery going on right under their noses.

Some very rich guy from Boston came here in 1880 or around then and built him a castle, just this side of the Afton Town line. It has turrets and battlements and all that stuff and about two acres of lawn behind a brick wall with a lodge and an iron gate set into it. That rich guy used to have twenty-five men cutting his grass, once a week, all at one time, so it would look like a carpet. Honest! You ought to go look at it.

But in the meantime that rich guy had died, and after lying empty for a while the place was sold to a stranger. Nobody knew where he came from, or why he came here. Had a foreign accent and a queer name, like Schellenberger, *Doctor* Schellenberger it was, though he didn't have any medical practice. All he had was that great big castle where he lived all alone. He couldn't get any help either, as people around here don't like waiting on other people. So pretty soon this young couple arrived from the other side. German, they were — I suppose like that old Doctor — and couldn't speak a word of English. That Doc didn't let them go out and learn any, either. Hermann Klepper was *his* name. He'd drive his wife up here to the store, and she'd just have to point at what she wanted and Ma would give it to her. Well, the old Doc worked them half to death. Hermann had to keep up ten acres of grounds, mow all the lawn, grow flowers and vegetables, and take care of the orchard. His wife had to do all the cleaning and washing and cook all the fancy meals.

Ankie and me used to help Ma in the store, weekends, while we were going to Junior College, and when Ankie found out Hermann didn't know any English and was fixed so he'd probably never learn any, he decided to help him. Hermann used to sneak up here Saturday nights, and Ankie bought a book with pictures in it — like, there'd be a picture of a hat and then the word "hat" beside it, and like that. That Hermann was one dumb Dutchman and Ankie'd finished pharmacy school by the time Herman could talk, I mean really talk, so as to carry on a conversation. One night when he left, Ankie was in a rage. "Do you know what your fine, upstanding Doctor has done to those two poor immigrants?" he asked me. "He's not *my* Doctor," I said, "but what's he done?"

"He brought them here and made slaves out of them!" Ankie meant just that. In ten years they'd never gotten one penny for all their work, and that Doctor Schellenberger told them they weren't entitled to any. They hated that castle and wanted to get away, but the Doc said they couldn't, because he'd have them deported — and by then Hitler had started the War, and — naturally! — they didn't want to go back to Germany.

Ankie explained how the Doc's not paying them was against the law, it's called peonage. Ankie was a fiery fellow in those days, though you might not believe it now, and was very influenced by Emmet McSorley. He got Hermann and Erna, that was his wife's name, all worked up, and he and Emmet lent them some cash — they packed up and cleared out of the castle and came up here to live, and Emmet helped them start suing the Doc for their back pay.

It wasn't long before the old Doc — he *was* old by then and had a bad leg too — kind of relented and gave them some money and begged them to come back. They said they wouldn't. So he said if they'd come back and take care of him in his old age, he'd leave them the castle and the lodge and all the acres in his will. "That'd be the day," I told them. But they did go back.

After a few months the old Doc began to get sick. It was his stomach. Lots of cramps and pains and couldn't keep his food down. Pretty soon he died.

And sure enough Hermann and Erna inherited the whole shooting-match. Much to everybody's amazement, it turned out the old Doc had some relations after all, a whole pack of nephews and nieces. And they descended on the place like a pack, I can tell you. Tried to break the will. But they never succeeded.

In the meantime, though, some people began to wonder about the Doc dying like that, so soon after he told the Kleppers about his will. He was decrepit, maybe, but never had been sick. Those relatives — naturally! — wondered the most, which finally led to an investigation, some detectives even came from Springfield. But the Doc had willed that his body was to be cremated and his ashes scattered over his acres, which Hermann and Erna'd done, so he couldn't be dug up and all that. So nothing ever came of the investigation. Only, from then on, some people didn't feel comfortable with the Kleppers. I always said Hermann was too much the dumb Dutchman to have thought of anything that much to his own advantage, much less carried it out, but others didn't agree. After a while there was a bad fire in part of the place. They got out all right, but pretty soon they went away. Nobody knows where, some say California, others say back to Germany...

A real estate speculator bought it — didn't pay much for it — and it lay derelict for more years than I could count. Now it's finally been bought — by some rich writer from New York City. They say he's getting it all fixed up, and gives great big drunken parties for his city pals on weekends. I'd like to go down and take a peek some Saturday night...

Wouldn't you think people would be more interested in the story that I just told you, something that happened right here? But no, they'd rather look at some Western on TV, if they've got a set. Otherwise all they do is gossip and sit on their backsides in that Italian-American Club and talk about money they haven't got. You can hear all these old guys around here tell about how much money some *other* old guy has got stashed away in his mattress, like the Old Barber will say old Toupence has got five thousand bills to sleep on and old Toupence will say old Ghitalla has six thousand, for instance. Don't you believe it. They're all dirt-poor. Old Ghitalla shot his wad buying the old Hebberd place, and now his son Johnny has got to work in that rundown barber shop the rest of his life to keep it up. The only one that's got any is me, and mine's in no mattress, but safe in a bank. I got it from smart ideas and hard work, and one of these days I'll put it to good use. And it won't be *here*. This is a crummy little town. What's that? As soon as I can unload this store onto somebody, then Ankie can sell his second-rate drugstore, and we'll light out for Las Vegas and open a high-class motel. Out there where the action is.

36. THE RICH WRITER

ROBERT EDMUND ROBERTSON

Sure, come on in. I don't usually see reporters without an appointment, but what the hell, I'm just camping out here anyhow, can't start writing anything till I get *one* room cleared out and get a table and chair in it. In fact, the only room where pieces of the ceiling don't fall on your head if you try to sit in it is the kitchen, so come on back there and we'll have a cup of coffee.

This way, down the hall. Don't trip over that stack of lumber. The kitchen's the room I fixed up first, as I like to cook and then sit around with some coffee and look out the window and wonder what in *hell* I'm doing here! See how sunny it is? Maybe this is where I'll work, as well as eat, cook, and just sit on my ass. Though I won't be able to do that much longer, as I've got a deadline with my publisher. He'll be up here any day now, nagging at me. Well, he can get a paintbrush stuck in *his* hot little hand too, like the rest of them. Don't ever write a bestseller, boy, because then every parasite in the world descends on you — they eat up your food, drink up your booze, borrow your dough without intending to pay it back — and then spend their useless lives talking dirt about you behind your back.

But I figured how to make them useful for once, and get rid of them at the same time. Every weekend when a bunch of them swarm up here, I just give them plaster and paint and say, "Come on, we'll fix up such-and-such a room this weekend. And no fixee, no eatee." So I get the rooms fixed, and that particular little bunch never comes back. By the time this place is finished, I'll be rid of the lot of them, and can live to myself the way I want to.

Sit down in the bay window here, gets the morning sun. Good looking window seat, huh? Built it myself. Made my living as a cabinet-maker part of the time, in the old days. Did my writing when I was out of work, or at night. That was in Pinecliff, the artists' colony over in the mountains on the *other* side of the Hudson. My wife and I were original members of the group that founded the colony. That's a lifetime ago, boy, and before you'd stopped wetting your pants. It was great there then, beautiful country, few people, woods all around your studio... All the rest were painters, working hard all day, didn't come around and talk your ear off when you were in the middle of a chapter. My wife liked it too — she made pottery — and our kids grew up there. It was a good life till the tourists and the hangers-on came. Then the place got crowded, cost of living went up, and the woods got sold for real estate development, as it's called, which only means a lot of noisy neighbors spoiling your view and your peace of mind. We sold that studio and built another one much higher up the mountain. It was tough in winter, getting ploughed out so as to take the kids to school and get to the store. But it was beautiful anyhow, and everything would've been all right if that novel I wrote about the President hadn't made it.

See, what happened in Pinecliff was that us "first settlers" kind of got our backs up against all the new people, and we became not only *old* guard, but very self-consciously *avant* garde. For instance, when the Playhouse was built, after the War, we'd put on plays ourselves in our Guild Hall up on the mountain. Cocteau or Beckett or that ilk. We rotated as to who played, who watched. Sort of mutual Backscratch-of-the-Month Club. And painters are lousy actors. But that way we boycotted the summer stock season. The interlopers, as we thought of them, didn't know what it meant to have to live through a winter up there — skimp and scrape to get canvas or work at odd jobs to keep your kids in galoshes. The new ones that really were artists had got it made. Younger than us, see, and made it in the post-war affluence and culture-pollution that was going on in New York — before they ever came to Pinecliff. They all had galleries, and enough dough to build Frank Lloyd Wright houses — or at least imitation ones — and swimming pools. And a lot of them had made that dough, working for *Fortune* or painting abstract shit in high-rise bank buildings, or as *illustrators*, for God's sake. Maybe part of our reaction was envy, but a lot of it really was integrity (damn the word!).

Well, sure we'd feel the pinpricks sometimes and get petty about it. See, if you're any good at your work, you usually know it. You never get *used* to getting passed over, you just try to go *on* working. But sometimes it gets too close to home: nobody likes to have a load of it land on their doorstep. I remember one time I 'went in our library, where my books — such as had been published — were conspicuously kept inconspicuously on a dark shelf in the stacks. Well, what the hell, I'd gotten used to that. But finally, after three years that stretch, there was a new one coming out, and I went in there to look through the trade papers and mags (that I couldn't afford to buy!) and see if maybe this time some snotty reviewer had given it a break. The librarian and her flat-chested helpers were all of a-twitter, greeted me with, "Mickey *Spillane* was just in here and autographed his new book for us! Want to see it?" "What's his autograph, an 'X'?" I asked them. But that made me feel as cheap as they were. All of our bunch had things like that, you know what I mean? And, well, God damn it, the finest one of us wasn't a painter but a sculptor — and you know what he had to carve in? *Wood!* Tree trunks were free, see, so that's what he worked in. Later on, that became real *chic*, pipsqueaks copying what he'd *had* to do — literally from hunger — found it paid them off. But he didn't live to get in on it. Hanged himself with his own clothes-line.

Besides those *illustrators*, the others that moved up there were just riff-raff, bourgeois chumps out for kicks — SEE 'EM WORK, SEE 'EM PLAY, REAL LIVE ARTISTS, COME ONE COME ALL. And also a lot of those parasites you get in the art world, gallery owners looking to add to their "stables," would-be patrons wanting a painter or writer to show off at cocktail parties.

So the more the place filled up with these types, the more old guard-avant garde *we* got. You could see our integrity showing all over the place, as conspicuous as the holes in our shoes. I personally wasn't so badly off, being an utterly unknown author. instead of a painter who'd got some kind of fame without money, and anyhow we by then lived off the beaten path. So when a few of the old bunch started to move away, upstate or even out West, we were satisfied to stay on. Might be there yet if it hadn't been for the goddam *President* novel.

So all of a sudden that was a hit. Sold a million copies in the end, bought right away by the movies — boy, was that a load of shit! — and I got rich and famous. The American dream. All the books I'd written before that had been remaindered were re-issued, all the ones that were still in boxes got published. Didn't matter whether anybody could understand them or not. At first it all seemed great — we had a lot of fun, went junketing to Europe, bought a few things we'd always wanted. But mainly went on living just as usual. Or tried to. But we weren't allowed to. Place crawling with photographers and reporters and autograph-hunters. (Some of them were kind of cute.) I was too dumb, or too unprepared, to know how to stop it. Should have just quit writing and told my goddam publisher to take his contract and stuff it.

But writing's an addiction like any other. And now I had the Midas touch. My wife couldn't take it. Left me. My sons, thank God, were grown up and out of my hair — got *their* hair out of mine, I might say. That's cut off now, to Madison Avenue page-boy style, as that's where they work. Yeah, that's how *they* turned out. No use harping on that, though.

The worst of everything was the night of the last meeting I ever went to at our Guild Hall. Once a month we'd always had discussion evenings there, even during the McCarthy days when some of us were in a lot of trouble, and others weren't, and there was a lot of dissension — well, that night for openers we had to talk about getting a new roof onto the building and how to raise the dough for it. So I offered to pay for the whole thing. I helped build the place, for God's sake — and what else could I do with my money?

You know what? They *booed* me. Then they yelled at me, things like, "You sold out," and "Go live someplace else," and "Resign, resign..." I just stood there and, believe me, cried.

That was when Eleanor had just left me too. So I thought, what the hell, I'll just go and *enjoy* my success in New York, do the whole bit. That city! — expensive slum, padded sewer. Lived there five years, too much inertia to get out. Drank too much, screwed around too much, felt like hell. Finally decided to come up here,

get myself some breathing space. I already knew this area — was
an usher once at the Music Festival. Got fired when they found
out my father was a Jew. (Changed his name during World War
One.) I bet I wouldn't have bought such a *big* place as this if it
hadn't been for that incident.

You never know, do you? Two little pin-pricks, like that day in
the Library and like getting fired up here when I was seventeen,
they led straight to New York and then up here. Or that's how
the head-shrinker works it out. But I must say I like it here,
though whether I won't get bored after I've fixed it all up, I can't
say. What the hell, I can always go off to Spain or Greece or
someplace.

I've got to get back to the cellar now and go on with the wiring
I'm putting in. Do you think that couple that inherited this white
elephant set fire to it for the insurance? Might be a good story
in that. I'll have to think about it.

Send me a copy of the interview when it comes out, will you?
Not a reporter? Well, whatever it is, good luck to you. My
gardener, the fellow that let you in the gates, can show you
around outside if that's what you want.

37. THE DITCH-DIGGER

"BUCK" MAZZEO

Didn't I see you, along the road, the first day you come here? Remember? — I was digging a ditch up there near the Pond.

Bet you're surprised to see me *here*, now, working for the Rich Writer! Yeah, I'm the gardener. *He* calls me Head Gardener. But there ain't much to be head of. All the help I got is two young guys, no better than kids and don't know a hoe from a rake. Don't know how to work. Not even *here* half the time, like today. And is this place a mess. Greenhouse, glass all broken. Driveway — and there's about a mile of it, like you saw already — full of weeds. Hedges all want clipping. Apple trees in the orchard all got scale. I'm going to start pruning them this morning. Perennial beds a jungle... Sometimes it just plain scares me, wondering if I can ever get the better of it. Of nature, I mean, who pays no mind to man's wants and wishes, and will take over the minute your back's turned. *Him* up there with his typewriter and his friends from New York City and his "do this, grow that" when it ain't the season for it, he don't know a thing. Wants tender plants grown outdoors, and seeds for vegetables planted in August. He gives me a lot of guff, all right, but I can take it. Just want to do a good job here. I got a right to be scared: it's my first real chance as a gardener.

Yeah, I set up in May, put an ad in the *Nickel Saver*, borrowed some money to buy me a jeep, and got me a lot of lawns to cut. But that ain't real gardening. Just pushing that power mower up and down, first one way, then the other. I still worked some for the town, ditch-digging, to make a little extra. (That's how you come to see me by the road, that day.) My wife works some, housework in Afton, but she can't make much because she has the kids to look after. It's not we need so much, but taxes is awful high here — seems like the more folks go away, the higher the taxes get — and you need a lot of warm clothes for the winters, especially for the kids...

This summer didn't bring in much. You get two and a quarter an hour here for grass cutting — have to have your own mower, too, and it better not break down! — and for road work you get two-fifty an hour. Get laid off when it rains, same as grass cutting, and in the dead of winter too. Winters I'd pick up a few bucks working in the greasepit in the big g'rage in Afton. I learnt that stuff in the army. But don't like it. Never did like machinery. Power mower's bad enough, but at least you're out in the air, and nobody can come and talk your ear off when you're mowing; gives a fellow a chance to be alone and think.

After I got out of the army, I went to work on the road-gang — they was building the Turnpike then, and there was plenty of work and even overtime. So I could get married. I got a piece of land from my Dad — he used to work in the quarry, though didn't get killed there like my brothers, but he's retired now and gone South — and built me a house, or part of one, it still ain't finished, as I often hear my wife say. — Sometimes she goes on something awful and I have to clout her one. — But after the Turnpike was finished, all I could get was ditch-digging for the Township. Never had enough education for nothing else. But I got muscles, as you can see. I may be small, but I got powerful what they call biceps — see? Got them beating up all them swamp Yankees that used to call us other kids wop Yankees. Well, as I was saying, that ditch-digging didn't bring in much, would never lead to nothing better, and we just couldn't get by. Everybody I grew up with — just about all the fellows I knew around here except Ernie Silvernail and Ben Stagliano — already found that out and had long since gone. Lot of factories moved from Melville and Hoosac down to Tennessee and North Carolina, so these fellows moved to the cities where those factories went. But I don't want no city — not for me or my kids. But by then my Dad, like I said, was South, way South, lives in a trailer near a beach in Mississippi. He was always writing about how there's plenty of work down there, like you'd say seasonal. So that year after the Turnpike was done and the snow came and I got laid off by the Town, I put the wife and kids in the old jalopy and we lit out for Mississippi. I stuck the family in my Dad's trailer and took off inland a ways where I heard they was hiring for tomato picking.

You maybe think we live poor here, but it's heaven on earth compared with what them migrant workers and sharecroppers live like down there. Now my Dad, see, was always against Unions and that stuff, and I'd never thought about it one way or the other. Going down there, that makes you think about it. It's not just the awful working conditions, it's you never got anything that's steady. One day sent here, the next there — in a truck, like as not, like cattle, kids in it too. Little kids working in the fields too. That's if you're a migrant. Sharecroppers don't have it much better. Can't call your house your own (more like a shack than a house, anyhow), always working somebody's else's ground — somebody that ain't even *there*, like as not — and what's more maybe today farming it, and the next day it's sold for logging or to some combine with all that machinery, and you're turned out. Black and white, brown too, all mixed together, and in the same boat. But instead of getting together, they're sworn enemies. I'll tell you, I'd never seen a black fellow before in my life, but I soon got over feeling funny working alongside some, only felt bad they had to live like that. I'll tell you something else, that fellow Chavez is right, even if he is what they call down there a Mex. I even sent him two bucks once. That's what my Dad and I had the big blow-up about: unions and organizing and all that. I guess we'd of been told to take ourselves out of his trailer, but I was ready to leave anyhow. I wanted to come home and have my kids be in a house they knew they could stay in.

So here we was, back again, and me back to ditch-digging, no better off than before, and like to stay that way. For I never had no education, like I told you, nor no chance to get one. But bad things turn out good sometimes, in a funny way.

First spring back here, a tractor hit me and broke my foot and mangled me up some. I was laying on my back in the Veterans Hospital in Albany for months with my leg in plaster and pulled up in the air on some pulleys. Seemed like one day was forever, like that — and there was a lot of days. The wife could only come to visit on Sundays, because she had to work. I'd never been one for reading. About all I could do in that line was get through a number of *Popular Mechanics* or some of those sexy books Ankie Varconi sells in his drugstore. Which were hardly the thing for a man with his leg in a cast...

One day Emmet McSorley come to visit me and brought me a whole batch of gardening magazines, books too. "Saw you pluckin the wildlings once, while you was supposed to be digging," he says, "so maybe these'll interest you."

Well, this here is the apple orchard. Good trees once, and I figure all they need is some treatment and a lot of pruning. See, they even still try to bear fruit... Now here's my ladder, my hooks and saws, and my tar for after. How much to prune? That's not so hard to figure: you prune out enough so that a robin can fly around through the branches. Yeah, there's a lot of things you can learn from birds and beasts, even insects, if you let yourself look.

Ayeh, I gobbled up them things Emmet McSorley brought me, told the wife to go to the liberry and get more. That's how I learnt gardening, and that's why you see me now here at the Big House, instead of 'longside the road. I aim to do the best I can and make a steady home for my kids.

38. THE SCHOOLGIRL & HER BROTHER

NICKIE & CLAUDIE GARAMOND

My mother's not home and my father's at the Union meeting.
Claudie and me, though, we're going to our house and have milk
and cookies, the way we always do after school.

I go to school too now. I go with Nickie every morning on the
school bus. My dog doesn't go to school. He has to stay here by
our bus stop and wait for us to come home.

Claudie doesn't really go to school. He only goes to kindergarten.
Because he's still a baby. I'm nine years old and in the fourth
grade. He only goes to kindergarten. Mother says... — You saw
me get off the bus that last day in June? I don't remember.

That was *summer*. Now it's fall. Father calls it autumn. Father
has a different way of talking, and he says my name different.
My name's the same as his: Claude Garamond, Junior. Only his
doesn't have Junior on it. Our name is like that because we're
French.

I'm not. I want to be Irish like mother. Mother is descended from
the Kings of Ireland. I changed my name from Nicolette to Nicky.
So the kids in school wouldn't make fun — and call *me* "Frenchy"
too.

My father's better than any old King. My father is a hero of
the French Re-sis-tance.

That's a long time ago, and now he's only a workman in the
limestone quarry.

In the winter when Father comes home he's all blue and red and
purple from the cold, but his hair is white from the lime dust.
He has to go to the cellar every night to brush the lime dust off,
and in the winter to put water on his face and hands besides.
It's called thawing out. It's so he won't get frost-bite.

159

So my name's Nicky, and his is Sticky. Nobody calls him Claude.
Except Father. Everybody calls him Sticky. Because of toads.
I tell him, if he keeps catching toads and carrying them around
in his hands, he'll get warts.

I *want* warts. But I never get any.

Mother went to the Bronx to visit Auntie Loretta. Mother always
lived in the Bronx — that's in New York City, were you ever
there? I was there once, another time that Mother went to visit
Auntie Loretta, before *he* was even born yet. But Auntie Loretta's
been in Ireland, and in Lourdes too. That's a place in France, but
not where Father came from. *She* wouldn't live in this backwoods.

Father says "Irish are priest-ridden." And it's not a backwoods.
It's good. It's where our house is. In summer you can fish off
the bridge over the stream in the Hollow. I fish with a worm on
a string. Father fishes with a pole and a long line and a thing
that pulls the line in when it's time. He casts the line up high,
it never catches in the trees. After it's rested on the water a
minute a fish bites and he pulls it in. Father catches lots of trout.
But Mother won't clean them. Father and I clean them, and my
dog gets the heads. I catch toads... Do you want to see my toad-
houses? I make them out of flower-pots. I'd show you my beans
that I planted beside Father's lettuce, but they're over now. I
can show you our ducks, though.

In the Bronx where Auntie Loretta lives, there's movie-houses
and super-markets, people all dressed up and in a hurry on the
streets. Or maybe sitting on benches in a park. Auntie Loretta
lives in a great big apartment house with an elevator. Sticky
doesn't even know what an elevator *is*.

Mother doesn't call me Sticky. She calls me Claudie.

And there's stores where you can buy clothes that aren't made
at home. This place is a *backwoods*. Mother says...

There's woods up on the mountain. My dog and I can run up nearly to the top. When we're hot and sweaty we lie down by my secret place, where water comes out of the ground and falls into a piece of marble like a dish with moss around the edge. The moss has little white flowers you can hardly see. My dog drinks with his tongue, but I can't get enough that way. I have to drink with my hands. The water's like ice-water and it cools you off.

Sticky *and* sweaty. Father says you have to raise your family in the country. Mother says...

Father says: Nickie don't be a telltale or he'll give you one on the ear.

Mother says we're only here because he can't get a job anyplace else. Except in this backwoods. Mother says that's what Auntie Loretta says...

In the winter there's not so much woods. Only pine trees and fir trees. Nickie and me, we have a sled. See that hill there behind our house? That's *our* hill. We haul the sled up there and when we get on and go down, we go faster than my dog can run, we go faster than flying.

Right now though it's fall. Some frost came and killed Mother's dahlias. They're all black. Mother cried... Father bought her a plant in a pot, but she says it's not the same. Mother says...

When it's fall I pick up maple leaves and try to draw them with my crayons. But there aren't enough different colors in the crayons.

Mother says we should go to California. When she comes back...

Is Mother ever coming back, Nickie? Did she go because Father doesn't really go to Union meetings? Like she said that night? Because he goes to visit the Postmaster's wife instead? Will she come back?

Mother promised...

Don't cry, Nickie. If you won't cry, you can play with my dried
snake's skin. Or you can show me those beads Auntie Loretta
sent you from Lourdes...

Then don't you cry either, Claudie. You go to school now, you're
not supposed to cry. — You'll have to excuse us, mister, because
we have to go in now and peel the potatoes for Father's dinner.
And make the house nice for Mother. For when she comes back.

For when she comes back, Nickie.

39. THE WATER DIVINER

ABEL CODWISE

When I was small, they used to call me The Natural.
There's an odd one in every old family — a black sheep
as they say, or a strange one the likes of Old Caleb
or maybe that young Luke, or one like me that's backward
in school and in the ways of other folks.
I could never learn to read or write, or to do my sums:
school was a misery. Teacher — that was Cornelius Silvernail
in them days — made me sit at a desk to one side,
sometimes made me wear a dunce's cap.
You may have heard of them things but I bet you never seen one!
The only other ones he treated mean was Prudence, my sister,
because she was by nature left-handed, and the Staglianos
because they couldn't speak no English. Howsomever,
the young ones weren't mean at all, in fact treated me friendly
and tried to help me. But every school-day hurt as bad
as the time I got my foot caught in a beartrap.
Only time I was happy was when teacher'd send me out of the
    room.
That was a mighty fine punishment. I'd sit on the doorstep
and look at the sky. Or I'd whittle. I was always
a good whittler and carver.
After they gave up and let me leave school, that's how I
earned my keep — making good things out of wood.

Reason they let me go was because I got so big. Even at twelve
I was the biggest in the school. Teacher'd say, All brawn
and no brains, but at long last he felt shamed to have me
setting there, so big and so backward. So then I set about
carving in earnest. But first I built me this cabin.
See, all these logs is hand-hewn.
I weren't big then as I am now of course — didn't have this
beard neither! — for there's nothing like wielding axe,
bucksaw and plane to give a man shoulders.

163

So here I've lived ever since. No, never married.
What would a woman want with the likes of me?
— Here's the snow-shoes I make and here are the bowls.
Folks find them useful.
These other things, statues I call them, though the city man
yonder, the Weaver we call 'im, says sculp-tures.

They ain't useful, but some find them pretty.
How my real work come about was by chance. One day I was
woods-walking and cut me a hazel wand. Don't rightly
recollect now for what purpose. Was then walking down-street,
peeling the wand as I went. Easy to peel as shucking a corn-ear.
And smooth, smooth. Was passing the old tenant house
Pierre Toupence had lately acquired with the sweat of his brow.
That flighty sister o' his didn't like the dug well,
didn't recollect how to pump, or mayhap didn't want to.
She'd got Arthur Tibbs, the Longyears' nephew, to move in
with his rig and start drilling. Chug-a-chug-CHUG,
chug-a-chug-CHUG, day after day, down to the limestone ridge.
Thirty dollars a foot, one place then another, day after day,
but no water. First mud, then rock, no water.
Louise greeted me most polite — she'd always done so,
I'll say that — and invited me back to gaze at that noisy rig.
So I rounded the fence and walked down the path, trailing
my peeled hazel switch. All of a sudden the switch come alive
in my hands. Twitched up and down, swung herself round,
I had to grasp with both hands to keep my feet steady.
She pointed up in the air and swung *me* around,
pulled me and pulled me towards other side o' the house,
'tother side from where the noisy rig was.
Then she began nosing around, hopped up and down,
drug me fast to one spot, and went still.

Pierre come along: Drill here, he shouted. He roared like a lion.
Tibbs merely laughed, but Pierre had his way.
And that's where they found water.

And that's how I found I was a dowser.

Dowser's the word they use hereabouts. Many knew what it was,
specially them from lands over the seas.
From then on I've been busy. More and more folks wanted
drilled wells that would run water into their sinks.
Tibbs would send some engineer fellow to look at the lay of the
land. Here's a good spot, he'd say — mayhap for no other
reason than the sake of convenience. But then folks'd say:
Send for the dowser.

My witch-hazel wand was never mistaken.

Now folks think they're smarter:
don't believe no more in old ways.
But even so they want me to come, if only for sport or,
like they say, quaintness. Or some think they'll be shamed
and bring me at night after dark.

But as I say the wand's never wrong. And so, do you see,
my life turned out good after all.

ABIGAIL'S DAYBOOKS

Excerpts from *Autumn, 1969*

September 29th. This mountain behind my back that sometimes seems to weigh me down with its stubborn mass, at others to lift me like a cedar waxwing's feather to its peak, has been the scene of many mysteries. The lights that flash in the night are not those of hunters, nor yet of Aurora Borealis (for these lights appear at any season, and not usually from the north); as they have no scientific explanation, I seldom admit their existence to anyone but myself... Above the spring where the mountain laurel grows, is where Emmet's father hanged himself from the oak tree, and the laurel did not grow for those many seasons afterwards. A little lower down is the cave in which Emmet found the abandoned infant boy who later returned to live out his life there among his pagan gods of tree and stream. And farther to the north, the strange cave Emmet and I once discovered, in the days when we still roamed the mountain together. Now, another mystery: eagles. For no reason a human being can fathom, a flock of these mighty predators has come to live in the remotest peak up there. I have seen them soaring, skimming the farthest blue, then diving, sheer, after their prey. Why should they come here, and how long will they stay?

This morning my thoughts turned to Prudence, a memory of her as a young girl, before she was married to her first love, then twice widowed; a girl with bare legs flying across a field and her hair flying in the wind — a memory called up by the traces of that girl which I still see in her today, and I sketched out a poem...

The Foal
(remembering Prudence)

Tacitus it was, perhaps, who said
'Iberian mares mate with the wind...'
On mountain-top, mane flying
she leaps, legs narrow as a colt's
prancing to excite, delicate, desiring;
Eyes slanted, hot with looking,
sun-dappled flanks she shows.
A light sweat at her arching neck
Scents that thin air, high
Where clouds form and heather grows,
A springing bed for her later pleasure,
And higher still she leaps
Until he sees, he smells, he sighs,
He comes with a gale's rush
And covers her, deep and down.
And she sinks, no longer
Prancing, quiet on the heather,
Mated now.
And I, when I shall be her foal,
I too will run
Upon the mountain-top
And seek the wind for mate.

Sitting near the spring where the deer come to drink, above
my outer pasture, I wrote and then looked over the other poems
written during this month. Now, sitting at my desk, beside the
window from where I can watch the sky for the eagles in their
distant gliding, I copy out my lines — to show them, perhaps or
perhaps not, to Emmet.

The results of this month's writing show that, with autumn,
memory is at work in me, yeast in the dough of my aging flesh,
autumn in my own autumn, they are memories I thought I had
forgotten... And some old recollections, as well, such as have not
occurred before: memories of *sounds*, so vivid that it's as though
I am hearing them.

Secret Flight

We'd heard it as a stretch
of hounds, belling after fox.
But above the frosted grass we saw
the sound was sketched on sky.
The wild geese, three days since,
like shuttlecocks, cork-floating,
had rested on Cobb's Pond.
Now charcoal wing-strokes
on the cloud, brushing distance,
inscribe a hidden journey, as hidden
in the locket of our breasts as in
those secret feathered breasts,
for a soundless winter's token.

Time Dissolving...

Time dissolves now
like bones thrown into lime.
Roots leave the ground
and a people their country.
Fruits wither and die in the dry earth.

The gossip carried malice
the child a gun
the priest an empty chalice
only the fading blooms
turned to the sun.

In these deserted gardens
the rose is overblown
and one humming-bird
hovering over bee-balm
drinks the autumn honey.

Killing-Frost

(for Pierre, lately)

Old man strong as a tree
Trunk upgrowing
Rooted in earth
Bends now, creaking
Over the earth:
Soil that he grew from
Seeded now by him.
Big splayed fingertips
Fumble small seeds
Into neat-drawn drills
One inch apart.
Earth then mulched with leaves and straw.
Small sprouts push out.
Another month and plants from
His seeds grow buds and bloom.
Carry water, then scratch
The earth to let in air.
Sun is like fire.
Corn goes to market
And an old man lives.
Evening comes sooner
The moon is colder,
And old limbs creak in the wind, saying,
There's frost in the air:
Cover the tender growth.
But in the morning
Green plants are black.
Dead stalks, rotten, drooping.
Now the old trunk bends:
Old man dies a little
With this other death.
Light the stove and wait now
For another spring.

At The Mountain

(a long-ago day with E---)

On this path near the summit
creeping pine grows in the shade
and deeper shade, cast by the mountain,
chills the ledge we stand on.

In a hidden cleft, whose
three kinds of damp moss
cinnamon fern and wood sorrel
grow against marble, a cave
is sealed by mountain laurel.

As we stoop to peer at a vixen's
tracks and through the leafy screen
into the warm and unmarked dimness
we must tremble: for we know
no human foot has stepped here
for a hundred years.

Yet we'll unseal this cave
to lie an hour and leave our traces
on this mossy ground
and a bed of bracken.

I am of two minds — or feelings — about the eagles. Even though
I was born here, I never got used to the preying of one species
on another. When I used to hear the great owl hooting in the
night, I would lie awake in dread for the sounds, terrible and
pitiful, made by his victim as he swoops down and tears its back
with his talons. The eagle, free and soaring — man's envy — is
pure beauty. Yet, yesterday, one dived down on Prudence's cat
and bore it away into the air, later, of course, to consume it. And
yesterday, also, that crass and fierce man, Obediah, shot one of
these great flyers. "I thought it was a hawk," he said. Was it the
same gun he used to shoot members of his *own* species, during
the war? And the final question: was the eagle less deadly than
the hawk?

40. THE CARPENTER

EMMET McSORLEY

It's a sad time: the leaves are falling and you, lad, like the birds, are departing. Though the birds of course do not take off for New York City. You don't want to stay in the city? Och, it was to be expected that your time here would unsettle you. It may be you've come up against more of the realities of living, here, than a man ever can in a city, especially in a sheltered place of learning *within* a city. It'd be hard to get a city-bred person to agree; however that may be, you've glimpsed an older way of life — or rather, its remnants. One that is fast passing. And whether that's good or bad, no one can say until later, when it's become history. At present, it's simply a fact, like a storm or a change of season.

I'd be the last to advise anyone. Time was, I chafed at the narrowness of this life, the shackles my work and my upbringing put on me. I wanted to get away — nobody but Abigail knows how much. My father wanted it for me, too, as well as for himself. He felt he'd been brought here by mere chance, and that no man's life should be ruled by that. But his solution came out of despair. You don't know perhaps that he hanged himself. He brooded over the quarry disaster, and he felt guilty too that — again by chance! — he'd been spared when the others weren't. My sort of brooding, in the darkness of winter, was different, had to do with the condition of all men, not merely my own. I say "was," for it's greatly improved of late. Though what's to come, I'd not be so bold as to try to foretell...

It was Abigail helped me out of the darkness. Not by her own personality, for her views are even bleaker than mine in some ways, but by the affection we feel each for the other. Indeed, lad, Abigail and I would have married. But Eph Dwiggins lingered so long in his illness, it was too late. By that time we'd both be-

171

come too set in our ways to want to mingle our lives to any
further extent. For instance, she's got the Yankee passion for
cleanliness, and I'm a sloppy Leinsterman. As soon as a dish is
dirty, she has to wash it. Whereas I leave mine in the sink till there
aren't any more in the cupboard. (As you saw when you came
to lodge here.) That's a trifling difference in preferences — until
a man and a woman come under the same roof. Then, too, we
have contradictory temperaments: I have a love of meeting people
and talking with them, whereas Abigail is much addicted to solitude. I used to take my manuscript in my lunchbox and scribble
in it quite easily, if need be, on a sidewalk bench, while Abigail
writes her journals and verses out in the woods. Besides which,
and most of all, Abigail's young love was Eph, that could never
be repeated, and her disappointment in him, later on, took the
fire out of her.

So why change what was good enough already? We were lovers
for twenty years, and will spend our old age in tender friendship.

Yet, even that devotion is not what kept me here... If it wouldn't
sound too highflown, I'd say it was the mystery at the core of each
one of us, and my curiosity about it. And that it takes more than
even a lifetime to unravel these things, beginning with a man's
own mystery. There are things you ask, about yourself and

others, that can never be answered. Even in the darkness of winter, I know there's still another answer, and another question.
But surely now, these things are inexpressible.

Let us just say: this was my home and so, eventually, I came to
see that I wanted to stay in it.

POSTLUDE

THE ROAD BACK TO THE CITY

Stonecrop: you could stay there for years and never be at home. But no place else will ever be home now, either. How do you find a place that's your home? unless you're born in it. Then, so many want to leave... The city: you can be born there, but never be at home. Never be able to put your roots through asphalt... "Old man, strong as a tree..." Narrow, uneducated old man, but something there, something you never knew existed. Emmet said: "The perversity of man and woman, the surprises we all contain!" And he said: "The mystery at the core of each one of us..." But at first you don't even know there is one...to let yourself realize that is the first painful discovery perhaps.

No, it won't do, now, to stay in the City. Or write some treatise about "small town people in a depressed area." (Was that really what it was going to be? — seems like another era, another world, another person: the time-before-Stonecrop). No, those people, those voices that won't ever stop now, would never let themselves be contained in a statistic. After all that, can't go back. But can't stay here. Someday, someplace...? But the roots in that some-place, they won't be an oak tree's, only those of a birch or a shrub. But something, anyhow. Only, where?

Look at the leaves! Red, bronze, yellow, but mostly red, burning in the cold air. Some falling now... Angie Sabato has oiled his scythe and put it away: he's in his barn now, building a new roof for his well. Mazzeo is inside the greenhouse, the glass and the benches restored, potting up begonias and other plants for a winter display. Emmet... Emmet is in his parlour, sitting by the stove to warm his

173

bones, reading the letters of Thomas Jefferson. There's Pierre Toupence's corn-field, with the plants blackened from frost. And there's the sign: New York Thruway, 22 Miles. And a dense grey cloud over Greystone Mountain that must have snow in it.

"It's autumn in the country I remember..." And soon, it will be dark.

CONTENTS